THE BASEBALL PLAYER

by

Thomas Carney

Wild Palms Press

ISBN: 978-0-578-02084-6

Wild Palms Press

Henry Birdsall sat on a pile of fallen plaster in one of the unused wings of Ellis Island, picking through scraps of old newspapers. The plaster lay on a floor of decomposing wood in a thick, vegetal rug. Ivy crawled through broken windows, the glass as thin and cloudy as human skin.

The Park Rangers, who ran the tours and administered the island, had probably dispatched a search party by now. Henry's fellow Cross & Case management consultants had left long ago, embarrassed to have visited in the first place. Back at the Manhattan ferry dock, Henry could imagine his boss, Ray Levin, whose idea this had been, staring across the water. The two other members of the Cross & Case team for the Armor Tech engagement would be loitering by the refreshment stand.

"Probably went back on an earlier boat, Ray."

"Great idea, though, Ray. Really it was."

An hour earlier, Henry had given the slip to the guided tour. While his colleagues listened to the Park Ranger recite his rote and, after that, to Levin apply these facts to the principles of management consulting, he had clambered through the remains of the island green house, the towers of the World Trade Center close enough to touch.

Presently, Henry could hear the voices of two Rangers, wearing the flat-brimmed hats of the National Park Service, treading through snowdrifts of corrupted plaster.

"We been looking for you," said the young male Ranger. "You shouldn't of left the tour."

"You got to sign papers," said the female Ranger.

Back at the Ranger Station, in one of the rooms underneath the Great Hall, Henry completed an accident form, stating nothing actionable had befallen him on his walkabout. The young male Ranger, Wesley, radioed to the larger station at

Liberty Island that the missing visitor had been found.

"So you been having work problems?" Wesley said.

"Problems?"

"Some work problems, you said."

"You mean union bribes?" said Henry. His consulting engagement with Armor Technical, a minority-owned firm fabricating military materiel in the Bronx, had suffered a recent moral complication: namely, bricks of cash spotted by Henry in an owner's briefcase.

The last boatload of visitors had now gathered at the ferry slip. The young female Ranger, June, had changed into a denim skirt and removed the gold name tag from her blouse. "Who you say you work for?" she asked.

"Cross & Case. Why?"

She smiled. "My brother's at Armor Tech."

"He is? What does he do?"

"Junior DeJesus. He's in Sales." Her blooming, taut figure seemed barely contained by her clothes.

"We're not supposed to talk about it, you know."

"Oh, yeah?" she said. "Why so?"

Henry took a deep breath. I am only the custodian of my education, he wanted to say, proof and victim of a long line of candlestick-makers become merchants and bankers, and finally poets and gentlemen inventors. But instead he said that management consultants were prized partly for their discretion, otherwise what would be the point.

"Sure. But that don't mean we can't talk about it. Just the fact you work there. You know, with my brother? So," she said. "You tired out from your walk."

"I am," he said, gladly.

She shuddered in revulsion. "See any rats?"

"Rats? No."

"You hear that, Roger?" called June over her shoulder, turning in a way that made the strap of her purse pull tight across the space between her breasts. "He say, 'rats' like he never heard of 'em? How'd you like to know, Mr. Cross & Case, there are how many rats, Roger?"

"Two hundred fifty thousand."

"A quarter million," she said, as though translating the figure for Henry.

"I didn't see any," he said.

"I don't see how not," she said.

"Where do you live," he asked.

"Long Island City. Queens. Know where that's at?"

"Sure. I used to play baseball over there."

She cocked her head, her black eyes less intense. His heart sank, but he plunged forward in a spiel as practiced as hers might have been giving the Ellis Island tour. He had played in the Puerto Rican leagues in Central Park.

"Well, what do you know," she said.

"Maybe your brother..."

"Naw," she said, "Junior don't go in for that."

The ferry finally arrived. As they moved out into the bay, the island warmth vanished. "You gonna be all right?" June asked, with not a little contempt.

He nodded, fighting against a familiar distress at having unspooled his baseball adventures to a perfect stranger. She looked at him and asked softly was he *sure* he was going to be okay. "Yeah," he confessed. "I'm a little lost, besides on the island." Henry prayed she could not see the sudden watering of his eye. But then he watched her melt.

"Gee," said June. "I'm sorry."

Henry wiped his eye, removing the cinder.

"Not your fault," he said.

In an old-style bar near the 59th Street subway, June had a drink with Henry. That she should not have been with Henry Birdseye or whatever his name was did not occur to her. She knew only that he was a man in pain and that she did not want to go home just yet. Also, she was attracted to his long-limbed differentness. His elbows, his brow-line and jaw seemed to have been drawn with a ruler. He was strange and "American," The Man from the North.

When they left the bar, the buildings seemed so close along Lexington that she felt overpowered. In the East Sixties, she glanced down the leafy town-housed side streets, hoping he lived in a brownstone like one of these. "My foot hurts," she said, which shut him up, momentarily, and allowed her to use his shoulder to balance herself while examining her foot. She had on nylons and her shoe strap had abraded a hole. "Now look what you've done."

"Jeez, I'm sorry."

The false concern in his tone she did not mind. What struck her was the way she caught him looking at her. Stark, appraising, male. His eyes widened when she twisted her body, getting her heel back in the shoe. In his smile gleamed a pleasantly animal aggression, which she liked.

She pouted. "I want to go home."

"I'll take you home," he said in a strong voice.

"Where you live?"

He lived in a building with a doorman. Not the kind of building she expected. An awning, yes, but the lobby was dingy. The Puerto Rican doorman, really an elevator guy, ran the two of them up to Henry's floor. Suddenly, she felt cheap. He does this all the time, she thought.

His apartment was dreadful. She glanced at his suit, thinking she might have been fooled by that, too, but it was good-quality, the sort bankers wore. She was in the process of drawing herself up, feeling taken advantage of, when he rose from the couch. "What would you like to drink?"

"I don't want nothing."

He went into his kitchen, anyway. Stood before the open refrigerator door, looking at a bottle of water, a six-pack of beer and a few cans of soup.

"What you got the soup in there for?" she said.

"I guess I don't need to. Want a beer?"

"Some water, maybe. You always live like this?"

Turning off the overhead light, he left the refrigerator door open so they could see each other while he poured two glasses of water. She decided that she would not sleep with him tonight. How could she in this pigsty. She could actually see the paths he took across his dusty rug.

"I'm gonna go home," she said in the living room.

He put his glass down. "Okay."

"For all I know, you married." Sure he was not, she said this big, so he could tell she was joking. "You kidnapped me."

"No, really, I haven't."

"You kidnapped me," she repeated.

Finally, he got the joke. "Yes, I have, haven't I?"

She stood up, arching her back so that everything stood out. And then, inspired, she stretched.

"You must be tired," he said. "I'll walk you down."

He put his hand on the back of her shoulder, pulled her firmly around and kissed her. Surprised, she suffered a quiver of alarm. She hoped he would not be rough, but he was kissing her with surprisingly full lips, kissing her softly and without too much tongue almost like a girl would kiss. He has done this a lot, she thought, after he pressed himself against her and led her by the hand into his pitch black bedroom.

The bed was a mattress and box-spring on the floor. No chair to drape her clothes over, which irritated her. What is the matter with these people, she snapped to herself. To him, she said, "I'm gonna go in the bathroom. Change."

Change into what. She did not wish him to see her in the

high-waisted cotton panties she was wearing. "And turn off the living room lights." She then racheted back on the bossiness. "Afterwards we going to sleep, right? Gimme your shirt." Shirtless, he looked vaguely silly with his watch still on.

"The bathroom is kind of a mess," he said.

Not messy, filthy. The grime on the tiny octagonal tiles forced her to stand barefoot on top of her shoes. Snapping off the light, she emerged into darkness.

"Over here," he said. "I'll guide you."

They crushed toes against each other and banged knees when he stood up. At one point he lost erection, and so lapped his penis against her vagina. They started talking and the next thing she knew he was in her.

He was ardent and physically good, but adrift in his own little world. She could tell he loved the touch of her skin because he groaned like he could not help himself. She sensed she was a little bigger in the hips and thighs than he expected. He was tall and square and sort of sharp, and he kept changing his grip on her ass. But he pushed at her, and he was long and he got harder and bigger when he came.

Over the next week, they got together twice, but the attempt to find common ground was fruitless and she did not care for a relationship based mostly on sex. Friendly and polite, he encouraged her to enumerate what she sought in a man. Both agreed that he presented quite a different laundry list. He had no plans to marry her, although he did remain open to being friends. The sex made that impossible, she said, given her emotional aims. And so she consigned her nights with him to the second-prize-is-experience bin.

That Henry Birdsall did not take his job seriously enough disturbed Ray Levin. Consulting firms like Cross & Case supplied fresh troops to a company in need: in theory battle-ready Hessians, but in practice eager kids just out of business school. The opportunity to commune with CEO's kept most of them too giddy with a sense of altitude and movement to realize they were basically wood chips plunging over a waterfall. Birdsall, however, had managed to mystify his superiors as to his career ambitions. Witness his disappearance last week on the Ellis Island field trip.

From the window of his 43nd floor office, Ray could see the ringed oval of Yankee Stadium. A few blocks beyond, his three consultants on the Armor Tech engagement would be rooting around on the machine shop floor, drinking coffee out of waxed paper cups and asking to see the books again for a particular month because they had forgotten to check an entry.

His intercom buzzed and Miss Smythe put Henry Birdsall through on the speaker phone. "We aren't doing these guys any good up here. The engagement stinks."

"Whoa, boy. You go through the proper channels on something like this. And you don't do it on the phone. We'll have a breakfast meeting."

"Christ, Ray, we had a breakfast meeting last week."

"So how's it going then?"

"The encyclopedia of job descriptions is useless. Half these people can't even tell us what they do. And now that we're figuring it out, we can't get it across to them what they're supposed to be doing."

"That's what you're there for."

"Ray, nobody's going to fire these people if they don't follow our suggestions."

"Never question the client. What else?" he said.

7

"Nothing. Just read the report."

"Have it right here." Ray said.

Flipping off the speaker switch, Ray let his feet crash down to the plastic rug guard. His team would be writing those job encyclopedias all summer at $2500 a day to Cross & Case.

A knock on his door. Arthur Tannenbaum.

Ray held up the report in his lap. "Armor Technical."

"The underwriters want a comfort letter."

"How come?"

"How come what?"

"I mean, sure. We can take care of that." When he talked to Arthur, Ray used short sentences, too, as though trying to imitate a bird call. "Bonds, right? How much they want?"

"Seventy-five mil."

"What do you hear from Bill Rayhill."

"Take care of that comfort letter. I assume you have everything you need. Saw him at the track," said Arthur.

Whenever necessary, Ray would bring up Rayhill's name to re-direct Tannenbaum's thoughts to his spiritually affirming friendship with the rotted-out WASP who headed the racing club to which Arthur belonged.

"So what's going on up there?" Arthur said at the door.

"Everything's fine."

Whatever Arthur knew about Armor Tech, Ray knew more. The company had problems in corporate purchasing. Contracts set up, but the work not being done. Big vendors dumping orders, small vendors not being paid. Armor Tech fabricated military materiel, which meant no-bid government minority contracts because the company was in the Bronx and hired people from the neighborhood and were wet-kissed constantly by the newspapers as a paragon of business initiative among the underclass. Cross & Case had received the typical mandate for a management consultant. Streamline billing procedures, write a job description manual and consult on what kind of computer system to install.

But there were a few loose ends, which no one knew about except Ray and Drew Case, a secret shareholder in Armor Tech.

Case was a name partner in Cross & Case, and the billings, which amounted to $50,000 a month, constituted nearly the entire justification of the firm's Long Island office, which was headed by Drew Case.

Ray took the train back to New Rochelle. He had gotten laid once, staying in town, by a divorcee in a red sweater whose poodle had peed on his underwear. "Damn you, Millicent," the woman had said, or maybe Millicent was *her* name, "you've wet the darn rug." Taut-faced, with delightfully slack skin, she had hoisted herself on the divan where they fucked instead of the bed and had stared at him full in the face until, blessedly, her eyes closed. "Don't wear any underwear," she said afterwards, tapping her cigarette with a long fingernail. "Or there's stores still open, buy another pair." She wanted him to stay the night, but he pretended to be taking the late train home, even though, quite erotically, she lay there with her pubic hair peeking out from under her robe. He returned to his Tudor City *pied-a-terre*, smelling of her and pleased with himself, and hand-wringingly guilty when he thought of his wife and two little girls. She had given him her number and a month later he called. "Who?" she asked. He told her. "Too late, you should have called weeks ago." And she hung up. Just like that.

Ray's wife, Dora, met him at the front door. "The girls are asleep. I almost came and got you in the car. I knew you had walked." She folded her arms, and in her high heels, backtracked like a shorebird towards the living room. "Dinner should've been ready twenty minutes ago."

Suddenly he was mortified not to have said goodnight to his little girls. Stifling the impulse to go bounding up the stairs, he tried to kiss Dora on the mouth. She turned her cheek to him. "I've been sampling the pesto. I taste like garlic."

"That's okay." He grabbed her awkwardly and pressed her to him, her hip impinging upon the softness of his paunch.

"Dinner in five minutes, Ray. Wash up."

A few nights later, Henry went to a dinner party on East 68th Street. At the table, his date, Susan Fehr, bracelets clanking, turned to him with an audible swish of blond hair. "What's going on with your baseball?"

"You mean softball?" said Bill Boyd, an antiques dealer.

"No," said Henry, smiling. "Baseball."

"He plays in the Puerto Rican league," said Susan, "with all Puerto Ricans."

"Here in New York?" asked Gary Pearse, who Henry knew from Princeton.

"He plays all the time," said Susan, mystified.

"Really?" said Bill. "And hardball, fast pitch?"

"Did you ever want to turn pro," Winkie Macklowe asked.

Lounging in his seat, Henry carved little skating turns in the tablecloth with his knife. "Not good enough. Although I've played with people down from Double A and Triple A, and it's not like you can't stay on the field with them."

"What's it like?" asked one of the women.

"I used to play in Queens with all Irish and Italians." Henry laughed, remembering a fight with another team, the murderous quickness of his teammates, the police cruisers, rolling over the outfield grass, careful as elephants, roof lights revolving silently.

"But what about the Puerto Ricans?" said Susan.

"Completely different."

"I see them sometimes," said Lane Cooris, "walking down the streets in their uniforms. You know, hats on backwards. And carrying those big radios."

"So what's it like?" asked Gary.

"What's it like? You're in the batter's box and a guy's cooking meat sticks over a trash barrel, smoke blowing through the backstop. Meanwhile, you're trying to hit. Gamblers in the stands are betting on balls and strikes, runs per inning. They got a PA system, big loudspeakers hooked up. The league president calls the whole game in Spanish and they think my name is Birdsong, so I get Birdsong this, Birdsong that. Opening Day, they play the national anthems of every country in the Caribbean. Which takes forever."

"How did you get involved in such a thing?"

Narrating his entry into the Spanish League, Henry felt a quaintness attach itself to his underclass hobby. He was not even that good a ballplayer. With his Anglo-god blondeness and size, he knew he disappointed the Puerto Ricans, who expected him to play the way he looked, enthralled as they were by their own racial stereotypes.

"I'm going to come watch, Birdsong," said Gary Pearse. "See if you're any good. Probably just a lot of bullshit."

"You should." Henry said, trying not to sound too eager.

Outside, the guests bid goodnight to each other in voices played out by cigarette smoke and alcohol. In the vest pocket park across the street civic illumination dispensed a snowy brilliance over a few huddled figures. "Looks like a drug deal," said one of the girls. Henry put Susan in a cab.

"Come on," she said, "I'll drop you."

Weld-intensity lighting extended like awnings out the windows of the fast-food stores as they rumbled up Third Avenue. "You want to get a drink somewhere?" he said.

"If you'd like."

"No? Well, okay. You can just drop me off."

"That'd be fine. A drink."

"What?"

"You want to have a drink, that's fine. Elaine's?"

"No," said Henry, sadly. "I mean, okay."

The yellow glow of the restaurant was too daunting, so they proceeded into a dimmer, more problematical night further up Second Avenue. He put his arm around her and she jiggled herself morbidly against him every few steps. They passed an insane woman with a shaved head and alarmingly visible stippling around around her nipples. They passed white couples in matching jeans: the girls with blunt boy's faces; the boys with fine soft hair combed back like badgers. Wherever they had been earlier that evening, they were not there now, and in the whopping severance New York can impose, they became as strange and unfortunate to each other as a pair of clowns.

"How about a cab," said Susan finally.

As they sped by his building, Henry managed to choke out the word, "Stop." He asked did she want to come up. When she demurred, he offered to drop *her* off.

"Goodnight, Henry," she said, sticking her hand between his knees. "You're not ready for me yet."

Angry and stunned, he got out of the cab.

In his apartment, elements of male insufficiency colored his desolation. To correct this, he read his prospectus for a floating parking garage. In his secret life as an entrepreneur, he had seized upon the proposition of cars parked in the bowels of a boat, the boat not going anywhere. His peers at Cross & Case made suggestions about liability, financing and legal pitfalls. When the day's heat vanished in the small hours before dawn, he stared at his reflection in a window pane, mesmerized by his own corporality.

Al Scoville had a labrador named Benji and a beagle named Al, a redundancy which amused his friends. A tall, square-shouldered black man, he had been a member of the original New York Browns, a CYO baseball team from Harlem. In a Brooklyn semi-pro league the young Browns had been clobbered by white powerhouses like the Coney Island Nathan's and the Park Slope B.P.O.E. Back to Harlem they had come to the field at 125th Street and First Avenue, where the crabgrass grew like a prairie fire and the left field fence was the Harlem River Drive. Al Scoville, however, hustling Al Scoville had stayed behind to play with the Nathans.

He could hit. It was as simple as that. He could see the ball and crush it. But during the years when he should have been signed to a pro contract like the whites on the Nathans, he was black, and after that, he was too old.

Al and the Browns reconnected on Long Island after demographic changes had reconstituted the team. Living with a woman now, Al had grown long and lank, his physiognomy elongated by disappointment. Every spring during the first few practices his arm would crack with adhesions breaking, then throb through the night. He had lost several steps and a yard off his throws, but he could still hit.

Although the Browns had replaced old Harold Ebert with a Spanish fireplug, Carmen Guitierrez, pompous and overly fussy about considerations like the colors of the team uniforms, Al ended up on a team with athletes whose abilities years later he could still recall. Sancho Bertelsman played first base; Tonio Gomez, shortstop; Alberto "Chango" Reyes, third. For a while, the second baseman was a black giant, Buck Beal. The outfield read Whitey Clarke, Al in left, and in center, German Soto, who played for the Toronto Blue Jays *after* his tour with the Browns. Pete Pierson, Harvey Little, a Dominican four shades darker than Al, and Hector Reyes, Chango's brother, pitched. Nick De La Torre was behind the plate. Others came and went, like Billy Gonzalez and Edwin Nunez, and the palmballer, Jimmy Lee. Marching through the Nassau Alliance, the team reached the semifinals of the American Amateur Baseball Association Finals being held that year on Long Island.

Al Scoville, whose dreaming life revolved around baseball, who moved through the rest of his life as though in a dream, could still not, six years later, accept what had happened to him there. The Browns lost 1-0 to the Levittown Giants, who became the National Champions in the next game by beating a Tucson, Arizona team. Al left three men on base, popping up twice, singling, flying out unheroically to right field. Nothing to gash one's chest about or tear out an eye, but the pitch he popped up behind second, with Nick De La Torre stranded on third, had been thrown years before on his first day on those sun-blasted fields in Canarsie when somehow, with all his talent, he had lacked the self-confidence to win.

Al played a few more years for the Browns, managing them in the Westchester Colonial League before the players started dropping away. With his two dogs clinking along beside him, he cut quite a figure in his pressed shirts and English walking shorts. As a member of Community Board 8, he cultivated an approachability which concealed the true chill of his personality. Residents of the neighborhood marked him as an emblem of New York remaking itself after the disasters of the 1970's.

Shiny-skinned and somber, his girlfriend Elizabeth left him periodically, experimenting briefly with a white stockbroker, undecided about how far he really wished to push his passions for jazz and soul food; and then, for several short stretches, with a woman, softer and fuzzier than herself, but ultimately too unformed. At the Riverside Neighborhood Association on the West Side, Elizabeth worked as a secretary/administrator.

Al had been a Community Board member for barely a year before a groundswell built to run him for City Council. Elizabeth marveled at his ascent and found reason to be protective of him. But while spearheading a Community Board fight against the overdevelopment of the Upper West Side, Al decided to resuscitate the Browns. The Herb Garden, a health food store he owned, had expanded into an adjacent storefront to become a cafe serving pastries and expressos.

At first, Al threw in with Rosey Malave, whose backer was a front for the pimps and drug dealers hanging out at a social club on 100th Street and Central Park West. Two Cubans, a shortstop and third baseman, and a surly, muscular Puerto Rican catcher gave the Browns' infield some tone. Then, through Eddie Perez, Al inherited a white kid who had played in the Queens Alliance. Tall and pretty nifty around the bag, the kid had a smooth left-handed stroke. For the first few weeks, Al thought maybe he really had something here. But Henry Birdsall tended to fizzle at the plate under pressure, although he always fielded his position well.

The Browns won the Coimbre Division of the Central Park Spanish League, but in a complicated play-off system had several games postponed, and then became disqualified for not having every player registered. Deciding to move the Browns back to the Colonial League, Al called the Cubans that winter, the surly catcher, and a Jamaican second baseman he knew, Leggy Smith. And he called Henry Birdsall, who he had forgiven for not being quite as good as he seemed.

The weekend of the Fourth of July, when Henry's parents asked him to come down for a picnic, the Browns had a game on Saturday and a doubleheader on the fourth. "You know," said his mother, testily, "you've always let your baseball come first."

"Look, if it's only one game, but it's two." He promised, though, to come down July fifth.

"Fine," said Guinivere. "You'll see Bobbie, at least."

He took the train to Ardmore, outside Philadelphia, and stood on the siding feeling a nervous insect-agitated peace descend. Wearing a racing cap and hunched over the wheel like Toad of Toad Hall, his father roared up in his vintage MG.

"We had a terrific time on the fourth," said Buster as they drove. "Your mother invited twenty people and plenty of kids for Ted and Elaine's kids. I didn't know we knew that many people here. It reminded me of when all of you were young."

"Sorry I missed it."

Pro forma, Buster said that everyone had missed him, too.

"How's Bobbie?. Still marrying that guy?"

Buster put on his long face rather than the eerily hopeful one Henry had expected. Bobbie was back on the sauce again and Lars had been replaced by someone named Craig. Beyond that, no hard news.

Bobbie, Henry's sister, walked outside when they arrived. Under a man's shirt, her halter top shirred horizontally across the mass of her breasts. As she hugged him, Henry had the unsettling but familiar sensation of confusing family warmth with sex. His sister glowed with election to sacrifice, an Aztec virgin diving into a blackwater pit of phosphorescing bones. "Give us a baby, Barbara," their mother, Guinivere, had pleaded once. "Just one. Give us something."

"Mother, you must be joking. That's so bald-faced." But

married twice and several times aborted, Barbara, the middle child, in arranging her life so as not to abandon her parents, had actually supplied them with a child, another child, a Bobbie, Jr., in effect.

"We don't have any other use for this room," said his mother, leading Henry downstairs. "So whenever you come, it can be yours." She addressed this to pillows to be plumped up, drawers to be opened for his belongings.

"Did you put Theodore and Elaine down here? I mean, where would the kids stay?"

She laughed bitterly. "They all stayed in a hotel."

"You're kidding?"

She grimaced. "I'm not."

Bobbie brought a girl to dinner named Ann, who revealed herself, upon inspection, to be button-mouthed and smooth of skin, pony-like to his sister's horse.

"And what do *you* do?" asked Buster, cardinally blunt.

"An interior decorator," said Ann, well-equipped for lying by a clear frank voice.

"Interior decorator," repeated Henry.

"Interesting," said Buster. "An interior decorator."

"Yes."

"How nice," said Henry's mother.

"Ann's from Philadelphia," said Bobbie. "Philly."

"Just don't call it Frisco," Henry joked.

Bobbie laughed. "Henry lives in New York."

Ann turned to him. "Really?"

"New Yawk." Now what?

"Phiwwy," said Ann.

"Interior decorator," said Buster, breaking into what he suspected was code. "You must be busy. Everyone I know is remodeling."

Guinivere stared at her husband. "Everyone *he* knows is remodeling? He doesn't know anyone here, and I'm not sure what remodeling has to do with any of this."

"Actually, mother," said Bobbie, "Ann is a contractor."

"A contractor?" Buster made the quick traverse from

irritation to perplexity.

"That's how we met," said Bobbie.

Henry could not resist. "Are you girls dating?"

Buster's eyes bulged as he started to speak. Ann laughed heartily, revealing her teeth. "Yes. And isn't it wonderful?"

Bobbie cackled. Henry grinned at Ann. Two beds downstairs, he was thinking, made into one. She grinned back.

The cook brought the silver service into the library, Buster having decided to watch a baseball game. Across the room, Guinivere, Bobbie and Ann huddled among the cups and spoons discussing a woman's place in the contracting world.

"So who wants to go out and get in trouble?"

Henry's mother gave him a bifurcated glance. Yes, with the girl, but not with Bobbie. Please, don't egg her on. Don't, damn you! "Or we could stay here," responded Henry.

"Can't," said Ann. "I have to be somewhere."

"No, you don't," said Bobbie.

Perhaps I *should* stay here, thought Henry.

"Can I borrow the car?" he said. His mother glared at him. His father glanced over from the TV.

The asphalt parking apron was cooling as Henry sat in Buster's MG. The front door opened and Bobbie and Ann came out, laughing. "What are you doing?" his sister asked.

"Waiting for Godot."

Neither girl said anything. He started to repeat the phrase, but with a different ending.

"Yeah," said Bobbie, "we heard that."

"What are you going to do about it," said Ann.

So many different retorts converged in Henry's mind that he could say nothing. The girls took this as mystery. "Follow us," said Bobbie, climbing into Ann's Porsche.

H enry and Ann ended up in the downstairs guest bedroom later that night. She was a chubby little monkey, which was in no way how he would have characterized her clothed. To come each time took him what seemed like hours, but she did not seem to mind and even hummed absentmindedly, rocking back and forth on him as against a vine. He woke up thinking he should marry her.

After she left he bearded Buster in his workroom. "You ever have union difficulties?"

"Sure," Buster said, rotating his jeweler's eyepiece to the top of his glasses, roughing out another perpetual motion toy.

"Payoffs, that kind of thing," said Henry.

"You mean to strike. Or not to strike."

"I actually saw one, I think. This Korean kid, the one I work with, Lawrence Park, we're asking Artie Machado about the figures for a certain month. He opens his briefcase: there's stacks of cash inside. So he answers our question, except now we got a bigger question. We don't say anything, me and Larry, until I ask him, 'Did you see that?' Yeah, he did. But, I mean, we're sophisticated, right? Because that's a lot of cash."

"So you went to your boss."

"We figured it had to be unions What else could it be? We're not a regulatory agency. And the partners don't like to know about any cash-in-a-briefcase shit."

"Henry, come on."

"Come on, what? See, this is what I wanted to ask you."

"It could be unions, but that doesn't mean you don't report it. It looks fishy, you report it. Pretty simple, right?"

"They do have union problems."

"I never knew a shop that didn't." At his work table, while searching out bits of mechanical gris-gris among his stuffs, Buster lay aside his cigar to apply 3-in-1 oil to his lips.

19

"What are you doing?"

"What am I doing? I'm looking for a loader spring, that's what. Oh, you mean, this?" He stared at his finger, glutinous with oil. "My lips are chapped."

Later, in the kitchen, Guinivere materialized. "I thought she seemed nice, Bobbie's friend. Quite, I don't know, poised. An interesting young woman."

To deflect her Henry said, "What've you been reading?"

"Sir Walter Scott. And I am amazed at his felicity. He is god-like in his odd shambling way wouldn't you say? Although I'm sure you've never read him."

"Yes, I have," he lied.

"Did you know his pigs followed him about, so sweet was the sound of his voice?"

"I did *not* know that."

"Well, they did," she said.

"So what about Bobbie?" They now stood in the living room with its gladey vertiginous view of tree midsections.

"What I don't understand," said his mother, "is her inconsistency. She's 32 years old, married twice, and she cannot for the life of her figure out what to do."

"Maybe Bobbie and I should live together. Boy, girl, man and wife, at home in the family home. What do you think?"

"I think I've had enough of you blaming me for your emotional difficulties?"

"Have you?" he said.

"I think I have."

"Okay, you have then. But don't tell me you actually want any of us to get married. Except maybe Theodore."

Buster, riding a bubble of inner joy, cast into the room. "Oh," he said, disappointed. "What's this?"

"Nothing," said Guinivere, beginning to cry.

With a sharp glance, which fell short of Henry by several feet, Buster took his wife in his arms.

"I can't stand it," she said.

"I'm sorry," said Henry.

"Go away," said Buster, his cigar erect between his teeth.

"All right."

"Stowaway," Buster repeated, "they found that stowaway. You know, who dropped out of the plane? He fell into the ocean. Spotter plane picked him up."

"Oh, yeah," said Henry, "that."

"It was on the news," said his father unhappily.

"The Indian guy."

"Pakistani," said his father.

"Into the ocean."

"Yes."

"He fell."

"Shut up!" said his mother. In consternation, Buster looked down at her, pressed against his chest.

"Okay, Guinivere," said her son, "I'll shut up."

"Not you. About the goddamned stowaway."

"So what's going on here, anyway?" said Buster.

"We've wanted to have this out for a long time, haven't we, Henry? We've wanted to... bash each other," said his mother, improbably.

"Well maybe not."

"Yes," she said, liking the idea, "*Bash* each other. So what I haven't liked all your girlfriends. Big. Fricking. Deal."

"You hated every one."

"I think they're idiots and that you're a fool. But not hate."

"You never thought that," said Buster.

"Don't tell me what I thought, for God's sake!"

"I think I'll leave," Henry said.

His mother compressed her lips. "You don't have to."

"Okay," said Buster cheerfully.

"Yes, I do," said Henry, "don't you see?"

"Back for dinner, though?" asked his father. "Or is that it for this trip?"

"Actually, I've worked up sort of an appetite."

Aghast, his mother stared at him.

"I'm hungry too," said his father, starting towards the kitchen and lunch.

Trying to expand to the maximum size allowed a no-bid minority government contractor, Armor Tech had decided to float a bond issue. The investment bankers doing the underwriting needed a "comfort letter" to assuage potential investors. As a fabricator of small gasoline engines, pontoons and the retractable ladders used in submarines, Armor Tech received numerous Department of Defense orders. Unadjusted revenues had been used to expand the company, creating more problems, but also more orders. Ray scheduled a breakfast meeting for his Armor Tech team.

For any purpose, apart from tying one on, Regan's was a bad choice, but Ray liked the place and chose not to register the dreadfulness of the food. "Can't we come up with somewhere else?" said Birdsall. "I had a knot of gristle the size of a quarter last time in my Irish bacon."

"Sit down there by Park," said Ray. "He's going to write the notes. You didn't do such a good job last time."

Birdsall had removed his suit jacket and rolled up his sleeves. "What do you mean I didn't do such a good job?"

Ray started to reply when he noticed a large bruise a few inches above Birdsall's wrist. "What happened to you?"

"Hit with a pitch. Fastball," he added proudly.

"So what's this?" said Larry Park. "You play baseball?"

Just then, Freddy Habyan arrived. A big boiled-looking Armenian from Chicago, unusually breast-obsessed, Freddy believed sex was the lifeline to the mother ship.

"I'm very pleased with the way things are proceeding at Armor Tech," said Ray. Despite the fact that I also feel you three might be getting too involved." He held up his finger to impart a maxim. "We don't feel sorry for, we fix."

"Yeah, but what are we fixing up there?" said Freddy. "Something that doesn't want to be fixed."

"I'm glad we are talking about this now. This is the time and place," he said, glancing pointedly at Henry, "to air grievances and doubts."

"Ray, the phones at Armor Tech aren't tapped."

"Look," said Freddy. "The whole deal stinks. I've seen these 8a no-bid deals before, and I'm telling you these guys can't be this incompetent."

"Yes they can," said Larry Park.

"We're doing an underwriting," said Ray.

"For how much?"

"Seventy-five mil."

"Which means a comfort letter. Whatever we give them will be cold comfort, let me tell you," said Freddy.

"So then tell me, exactly," said Ray, "why all of you feel it's so hopeless. A new computer system and a way of blowing up that logjam in corporate purchasing. And gradually a way of slowing down revenue recognition to keep the General Ledger in step with cost assessments. We know what's wrong."

"When's the letter?"

"Three weeks is the red herring. Listen, we have a president in the White House spending more money on defense than God did making the universe, and these guys are getting orders, Jesus, I see those figures. Where's the spirit? I got a great team here. Birdsall knows the floor, we got Larry working accounts, and a senior manager on financials. We can do a job for this company. We are doing a job. Come on."

"These guys ain't that smart, Ray," said Freddy.

"Stupid," said Birdsall, "and taking some big chances.

"Then let's teach them something."

From the Armor Tech parking lot, Ray could hear the thumping of the machine presses muffled by the tin-looking barn, its tiny paned windows opened for ventilation in great shoals. Ray and the others climbed the loading dock into a scrim of shadow so sudden he felt chilled. "You want to see the yarmulke kid?" said Birdsall. "Hess, the accountant."

"Let's go over to pontoons," said Ray.

Noxious light buzzed from the trays of fluorescents.

Gloom swung like a curtain, changing its gyre as they approached. The pin-up girls with scribbles of appreciation on their asses and tits, the wanton, silly sluttiness of the girls themselves, all this thrilled Levin with a sense of trespass.

Donald Lopate, wire-rimmed glasses lending steeliness to his mouth and eyes, looked up in his office from a print-out sheaf. "What's doing, Ray?"

"Not much, Don, except my guys here are having trouble getting what they need."

"And what's that?"

"Park and Birdsall can't chip anything out of Marshall Hess on the payroll figures and the pension plan."

"I'm the one told Marshall keep that stuff to himself. I figured what you don't need, you don't need, right?" Lopate turned to Freddy. "So, how you doing thus far?"

Freddy exhaled. "Good."

"You working closely with Artie, or what?"

"Or what," said Freddy.

"Let's get him in here. Arturo," he called.

"You know, Mr. Lopate, we should have asked, but we never did," Birdsall said. "Do you have union problems?"

"Union problems? Of course we do. Everybody does."

Birdsall and Larry Park exchanged glances.

Upon being apprised of the accounting difficulties, Arturo Machado whined, "They can't find this stuff? What the hell I tell everyone cooperate for? Huh? Veranda, get in here… You tell sales, accounts, production. The hell with it: tell Bobby, Hector and Richie. Tell 'em I want 'em in my office, 10:30. And I don't want no excuses."

"So then let's get our heads together," said Ray, mortally depressed, "on this comfort letter."

"**S**ometimes," Al Scoville told Elizabeth as they lay on his fold-out sofa bed, "I want to send flowers to myself after a real tough loss."

"I'll send you flowers," she said, huskily.

"Everything seems to stop after a real bad loss."

She reached for a cigarette. Snapped the match dark. "But you won this afternoon," she said.

"Six for eight," said Al. "A good day."

A week flashed by in a hand-clap. Never quite sure where these weeks went, Al found his year ended when the weather got warm and only started up again in the full crispness of fall. Baseball lobotomized him. Afternoon would arrive, the hands of the clock assuming the complicity of an inside joke. A splice would occur in his waking hours, and again he would be pulling his equipment cart down West 96th Street. Searching out an area of grass in which to practice, he would be nagged by the possibility of the sun going down before he could plunge his hand into the sinecure of his glove, throw and then hit the ball. Al Scoville, Community Board 8 member, did not have, and had never had, as a player, manager or owner of the New York Browns, a field permit.

"How hard can it be to get one?" Elizabeth asked. "You go down to the Parks Department. You say, I'm Famous Al Scoville or whatever you politicians say to each other, and they go, 'Oh, shit, what a mistake, just give us a folded $20 back with this form and the field is yours.' Come on, Al, don't be so ragtag, please, so 'negro.' Get the damn permit, so I don't have to hear how you gotta be out there early to get a good field."

At practice on Fridays, seated on a vandalized dugout bench, Al would knock his spikes mudclot free, fold his pancake feet into them. Snatch his clothy glove from the cart, and a seamy concentrated ball. Creak his long arm around in its socket, move out onto the infield with exact little *plie* steps. That first painful flip of the ball, its simple motion, from here to there. Back and forth, he would throw, often with Birdsall, then shuffle out to the mound to pitch batting practice.

"Okay, lay down a few. Ten swings and out."

Whizzing past his ear, the scythe of his arm, the darting obedience of the thrown object. He had read somewhere that certain skeletons of ancient man had abnormally developed forearms. They had been the throwers, archeologists reasoned, early athletes in the game of hunting, the long range killers. He would pitch until his arm was loose and then hit. Pushing his feet through the pocked, unresistant dirt, he would assume a stance so knowable that pitchers immediately knew he could hit. At times, Elizabeth, who rarely went to see him play, would think, watching him chose his pitch and swing, that no Al existed beyond this one.

After he hit, he would slap grounders to the infielders.

"That's what I'm talking about. Don't turn your wrist over like that. Makes you come up too fast." Almost 40 years old, he marveled at how the desire to engage had changed for ground balls. He remembered the ballplayers of his youth snatching up dirt and pebbles to be exuded like rifle smoke when they threw. These kids today played as though dressed in party clothes. "Get down, goddamn it. Let it hit you in the face," he would say. Meanwhile, his players would stare at him, thinking, this guy's lame.

"I feel," he said to Elizabeth, "like a damn dinosaur. Because I saw the way the game was played. These ones now? They make plays guys I grew up with never would have made. And then fuck up the easy ones."

"Culturization," said Elizabeth, who had her own frame of reference at the community center. "Learning to put the two things, the natural and the learned, together."

Bang! the ball would skitter into the light from the shade where Al stood with the fungo bat. It would hop lively towards a kid who would snap the ball up, wrist turned inside out, glove hanging upside down, the ball, though, inside. Wrong, but beautiful. "Okay," Al would have to say. "Fine."

In the long afternoon shadows, the Browns would hit until their hands reddened, showering balls into the ocean of outfield grass. Whatever heat had gathered for the day would be dispersed and Al and the others would become as characteristic of evening's arrival as cows headed for the barn; as birds, wing folded, nestled in the branches; as dew. Al would collect his dogs and the materials of play. His players, as they had appeared, would depart, dinners awaiting them, wives, dates, lonely rooms. The Park would empty, except for the proverbial jogger, the lamplighter, streetlights blinking to life as he passed. A convocation of heat and darkness would rise from the ground and the Park would take on its deadly oddly inviting nightliness. People in going-out clothes would be rushing along 96th Street. The air-conditioners, the traffic, the subway rumbling beneath the ground would arrange a sound which to Al signified summer: a great open-throated roar.

He would quicken into his building's vestibule, into its groaning clicking elevator, his dogs in an existential daze. Great racket in the cramped foyer of collar buckles chinking against wire laundry cart, clunking of bats, but now he was home and she was, too, and tomorrow meant a ballgame. "Hurry up," she would say. "What you waiting for, boy?"

"For you."

"I'm ready!"

Downstairs now to the bar on the corner, the Adage Lounge, for cocktails and merriment. Rare the summer evening when she was out of sorts. And after she had been asleep for hours and only an earthquake could pile him on top of her again, Al would be thinking baseball.

That fall, at a French restaurant in New Rochelle, Dora, Ray's wife, asked why he seemed particularly dour tonight. "The Armor Tech engagement," he said, "is having a few problems."

"*'Qu'sque 'cest*," she asked the waiter.

"*C'est les rognons de veau, madame*," said he.

"So what's this about Armor Tech," she asked, confusing the waiter who thought she was talking to him.

"Nothing," Ray said grimly.

"The stock thing didn't work out?"

"How was cooking class?"

"You know what these are, don't you? Kidneys, yuck."

"It fell through," said Ray. "Fastest crater ever. Seventy five million worth of debt and nobody buys a penny."

Ten days earlier, Drew Case had said, "The Engagement Report they want, but no implementation." Like a forest, smooth WASPy hair encroached on the small clearing that constituted Case's forehead. "It's finished, right? The report?"

"Of course."

Actually, of course not. A speaker phone conversation during the composition of the comfort letter had trigered a slight morale problem.

"Donny? Marshall?"

"We're here."

"We're here, too. Myself, Freddy Habyan, Birdsall. You know Larry Park."

"The Korean," said Hess gracelessly.

Park smirked. Birdsall mimed Hess tilting his yarmulke back like a cowboy hat. The numbers on production quotas and recorded revenues were run through. Finally, Freddy Habyan interrupted the drone. "These are all correct?"

The speaker phone crackled emptily for a moment.

"Yeah. They are," said Hess.

"Of course they are," said Ray.

"No, really, they are, aren't they?" Habyan persisted.

"They're correct," said Lopate. "Completely correct."

Park threw down his pencil, triumphantly. Birdsall shook his head. Freddy flopped back in his chair like a bag of wheat. Quelling a move on Lopate's part to finish tonight, Ray maneuvered the speaker phone quiet. Turned to his three.

"No comfort," said Habyan.

"I think we just waste a lot of time," said Park.

"He's lying, Ray. Were you listening to the guy?"

As a matter of fact, no. Ray had been listening to Drew Case, to the hammocks and honks of his Oyster Bay accent. This was a call to honor. "We know how the deal is structured and what we need," he said. "This is debt, remember? Bonds. Let's take a break, I got to call my wife."

Freddy stalked out of the room.

"Why don't you put her on speaker phone?" said Birdsall.

"What time is it?" he said to his wife.

"Don't you have a watch?"

"What I mean is, if it's seven o'clock I think I can get the eight ten home."

"Are those poor jerks still there with you?"

"Almost done," said Ray, diving to switch off the speaker.

A week later, the Armor Technical bond underwriting blew up in the oven. The stock price careened wildly downward and the Bronx-based fabricator began to explore Chapter 11 possibilities. By then Cross & Case was bulletproof, having pointed out what was wrong with the company, even before the Small Business Administration took away its minority business designation.

"We warned them about recognizing revenues too fast," said Arthur Tannenbaum, glancing up from Levin's desk where the *Daily News* lay open to a nasty Armor Tech headline.

"I know," said Ray.

Shrugging, Tannenbaum wet his finger, flipped to the racing section. "How's Rayhill?"

Tannenbaum eyed him. "We got no business with these kinds of people. I was against it from the start. And you can tell that to your friend, Drew Case."

"Arthur, the bond issue was supported by the figures. We don't know what went on in Washington."

"Meaning?"

"That this stuff about lobbying and influence peddling? It could go all the way to the Kremlin, but it doesn't take away from the job we did."

As the Armor Tech story sparked and died and sparked again, creeping through the media like a controlled forest fire, Ray came under scrutiny within the firm. When allegations surfaced that Lopate and Machado had used shares of company stock to pay off the law firms of local Congressmen, Mike Peruwitz, the division chief, popped his head in one morning.

"They got you good, Ray. Get 'em back."

That afternoon, Drew Case dropped by. "A drink?"

"When?"

"Now."

"Good evening, sir," said the Chinese maitre'd. It was, by Ray's watch, 3:30 pm.

As Drew Case bottoms-upped a scotch, Ray said, "You're safe, I assume."

"Did I get out?" Case tossed the menu aside. "Two weeks ago." To the waiter he tapped the rim of his glass. "They're putting on prosecutors."

"State, that sort of thing?"

"Federal. And announcing probes. I don't know what they're looking for. Thank you." A second scotch had been placed in front of Case. "It's ridiculous. We consult for a firm in trouble, tell them they're in trouble. And they turn out to be in a lot more trouble than we knew."

"How important is our comfort letter going to be?"

"That's not our problem."

"What is?"

Case smiled. "Actually, nothing is. All problems are now the sole property of Armor Tech. They subpoena our records?

So what. We have no worries with that."

"How about Lopate? Anyone know the connection?"

"No one knows. Not even you."

Ray laughed, awash with a bashful reverence for Drew Case, who then pulled a rubber mask out of his pocket. "Want to go to a party?"

"Halloween?"

"Tomorrow, I think. What's today, Thursday?"

Ray took a gulp of his drink. "A Halloween party? Sure." He looked at his watch. A balance of Dora and the children presented itself against the sudden snugness of the Chinese restaurant. "Let's go," he said, grabbing the check.

Leaving the restaurant, they waded across rivers of dead light towards the plunging sun. Stopped in phone booths to phone secretaries and wives, or not to phone them on second thought, in Ray's case, clicking his quarter along the metal articulated cord. Eventually, they took a cab west toward the rotting docks and union offices, the concrete plants and vestigial Irish bars. Into one of these they went.

Ray could hear the trollies of old New York, certainly the elevated trains, could smell the horse-shit gathering outside the door. Light rammed its way through the gummy windows and voices heard in the street had the challenge of God.

"What's the name of this place," he breathed to Case.

"Dean's."

The new courthouse reporter from the *Times* that January, a tall blond guy, appeared to have only the shakiest grasp of his craft. "You're the AAG handling the Armor Tech case?" he said to Sarah Mortensen. "There any way you could let me see the relevant materials? Non-sensitive, of course."

Robert Abrams, the New York State Attorney General had just changed suites and many of Sarah's files remained in boxes. Leafing through the preliminary hearing paperwork, she mulled over what she could let a reporter see.

"What's going on?" she asked.

"We think it's a good story. Here's this little outfit in broken-brick-ville. They get their big start in life and everyone says, 'Imagine that, the South Bronx.' And then bam!, it's over, the guys are crooks. Or what looks like crooks."

"Does the *Times* think they're crooks."

"I don't know what they think. What do *you* think?"

"Off-the-record, you mean? Any quotes have to go through Public Relations."

"Sure. Off-the-record's fine. So these guys are crooks, but how far beyond them does it go? And is anybody, how do I put this, sharpening their sword?"

"Anybody?"

He sighed. "Bob Abrams. I know you're not going to tell me, but tell me anyway."

She smiled, amused by his purposeful naivete. "We think the case might lead to other cases. Further up the ladder."

"Sarah," called her paralegal. "The boss."

"You may have to leave," she said, picking up the phone. Her conversation with Bob Abrams, though, was short. A few grunts of assent on her part to grunted requests on his. She hung up and then allowed the reporter to read a deposition she had not copied.

He whistled between his teeth. "Stock fraud, too?"

She now revealed to him her scheduled departure, later this month, from the State's Attorney General's office. She had taken a job in the private sector at Shea, Gould.

"Sorry," she said, handing him her card.

After he left, she reviewed, as she occasionally did, what she referred to as her "sequence of steps." These began with her slender girlhood at the Emma Willard school, ascended to her plunge down the narrowing flue of college and law school, and ended with her leap to her emotional death from this high windy place in the Trade Towers. From law school she had gone to work for a Special Prosecutor. Acquitting herself well in the nursing home trials, she had been approached by Liz Holtzman, famously lesbian, to work in the Brooklyn D.A.'s office, an offer from which she recoiled.

Lying in bed, digital clock paddling digit by digit towards dawn, she had eventually grasped the immensity of the cliff she clung to. Dowdiness had taken title to her and in a 19th century French ironic way she had become what she despised. Shea, Gould had hired her because she embodied that old reversal of expectations gag: the toughest one of all, and she looks like a school teacher.

When she left work the evening had turned arctic bright. She had a destination tonight, a get-together at an Irish bar, but having misplaced the coordinates, she stood at the base of the Trade Towers, reluctant to brave the boxcar elevators back up to her office on the 78th floor.

On the train, studying a Miss Subway poster artistically enhanced by pen-and-ink additions of male genitalia to the young woman's nose, mouth and ears, she remembered part of the address and resolved to find the place by walking up Eleventh Avenue. The sidewalk glittered and crunched. Her singleness against the superfluity of cars struck her as true. In a trance of recognition, she drifted into a bar. The bartender asked what she was having tonight, his blue-black hair combed back in thick tines. Into a glass he glugged whiskey from a green pouring beak that seemed so ethnically correct she wondered were they always green.

"Sarah!" It was Judy. "So glad you could come."

Short and busty like Sarah, but not drab, Judy negotiated an alley between bodies at the bar. "I want you to meet Drew and Ray. They're regulars here."

"Hello, Drew," said Sarah, instantly forgetting the man.

"Hello," said Drew Case.

"Sarah, say hello to Ray," Judy said.

By early April, Sarah Mortensen had her feet under her at Shea, Gould. "But all I'm doing," she told her mother, "is taking money out of the pocket of one rich guy and putting it in the pocket of another."

Slightly uncomfortable with her changed circumstances, she found herself drawn back periodically to Dean's, and to her friend, Ray Levin. "Still working on the Armor Tech story," she asked the young man at a table with Ray and a preppy-looking college girl.

"Fuck!" said the young man.

Ray stared at Sarah. "What story?"

"Is he interviewing you? You know you can go to jail for that," she said to the young man.

"Oh, Christ!" said Ray, nervously.

Sarah did a double-take when she realized who the girl was: Rebecca Van Rijn. Old New York family, terrifically rich, and because of her dead parents' fame, her name, and occasionally even her picture, showed up in the gossip columns.

"Henry," said Rebecca Van Rijn, "what did you do?"

"He pretended to be a *Times* reporter on the Armor Tech story. Hold on," said Sarah to Ray, "you two work together, don't you?" Ray put his head in his hands.

"Honestly," said Henry. "I was just curious."

"You and I... Henry? Is that your name? We need to have a little talk about this."

"You want back what you gave me?" he said.

"What did you give him?" said Ray, alarmed.

"Nothing sensitive, obviously."

"When are visiting hours? Maybe I'll come see you," said Ms. Van Rijn. "Although not more than twice a month, okay?"

"So how do you two know each other," Henry asked.

"Drew Case dragged me over here." Ray turned to Sarah.

"You had just moved to Shea, Gould."

"After being interviewed by Jimmy Olson here, yeah."

"How'd I do?"

"Shea, Gould, the law firm?" Rebecca perked up. "Do you know Myron Kandel?"

"I've met him."

"He's my grandfather's lawyer."

"Rebecca wants to be a lawyer," said Henry.

"But first I want to bet baseball games."

When Henry and the Van Rijn girl got up to phone in their bets, Sarah turned to Ray.

"No, I don't," he said. "I don't know how he met her. But is he *criminally* stupid, I'm asking myself?"

"He is if he passed on material to the defense counsel."

"I should probably fire him. But instead of that." Ray drained his bourbon. "Instead of that, I'm giving him another assignment. Court-appointed, too."

"A compliance order?"

"On a concrete company appealing a judgment. This big colorful Irish palooka, Richard Fitzgerald. Dicko, they call him. A City suit."

"You're putting him on alone?"

"The guy he was under, Freddy Habyan, is now my boss. Yeah, alone. He's supposed to monitor ledgers. Make 'em stay kosher on the counts they're not appealing."

"Ray, am I going to be embarrassed? These Armor Tech indictments. They have two congressmen taking stock gifts to their law firms. I see names involved like Lyn Nofsinger and Ed Meese. Am I going to see yours?"

"We got paid too much for what we did. Cash, though, not stock. So, yeah, I might have to testify."

Henry and the Van Rijn girl came back to the table. She had freckles, dark hair, and a lovely largeness of feature. While Sarah could savor this moment of random connectedness, the sight of that bluish Irishman somberly wiping down his bar reminded her of a loneliness she knew she would always know. Every gathering eventually reduced to a solitude of one.

Ray left to catch his train. Sarah shared a cab with Henry and Rebecca, then walked along her street under the spindly budding trees revisiting the night she had ended up in midtown with Ray, outside his *pied-a-terre*.

"Want to come up?" he asked her. They were in front of his building in Tudor City. Physically, Ray was a solid doughy guy with a brushy head of hair. "Or we could have a drink down at the corner." A pang went through Sarah. Ray Levin was all she was going to get. A married man with two kids and a strangely deep allegiance to his job. The Mr. Chips of Cross & Case. She climbed out of the cab. This was the moment when she became truly unafraid of all consequence.

"Except I'm out of booze," Ray said, walking her past his vestibule, "so we'll go down to Tangerine's instead. You never come over here, do you, to the East Side?" He was going to keep babbling until she said something.

"Fine."

Clumsily, he gave her a hug as they pegged down the incline towards the bar. He was thanking her for having seen what he saw: his doorman in a winter greatcoat and braided cap drifting out from the lighted warmth of the building. His doorman, who would have opened the door and said as they whooshed past, "Good night, Mr. Levin;" and who would then be saying, "Good afternoon," "Good evening" and "Good night" to Mrs. Levin until his employment contract ran out.

At Tangerine's they sat on barstools that heaved and rocked with second thoughts, but then steadied after a drink or two. When Ray put her in a cab, he kissed her on both cheeks. "That's how the French do it."

"*Certainment*," said Sarah, kissing him on the lips before the cab whisked her off through the First Avenue steam trails.

"**D**o you like to kiss?" asked Rebecca.

She was leaning into the crook of his arm in the back seat of the cab. She turned her face up so he kissed her. She was still seeking solutions to the lips/ teeth problem and having trouble with this concept: soft mouth.

"How was that," she said.

"Better."

As usual, she had forgotten her key and had to ring the doorbell. Harriet, her old governess, who was, in fact, not very old, hissed out to the door in mules and a bathrobe, swung the door open, smiled at Henry, frowned at Rebecca, and then slip-slid back to her quarters across the herringboned floor of the Park Avenue apartment. "Sorry, Harriet."

"Then do not do this."

Rebecca disappeared into a room Henry knew as the library. He now heard a voice. Not hers. His heart sank and his pace slowed, but he plunged on. Grandmother Priscilla Van Rijn sat in a damask chair, half-glasses on her nose, reading a leather-bound book. Lowering the book, she glanced up at Rebecca. Then over her glasses at Henry.

"Was that you ringing the buzzer?" she asked Rebecca.

"You met Henry, grandmother. He's teaching me how to gamble. We have the Cardinals over the Giants tonight at five-and-a-half/six-and-a-half."

"Rebecca!" said Mrs. Van Rijn mildly. Then to Henry," Does she have any idea what she's talking about?"

"Unfortunately, she does."

"Well, I was just going to bed," said Mrs. Van Rijn.

"No you weren't," said Rebecca.

"So I'll leave you two," she said.

Henry actually liked Mrs. Van Rijn, whose open, friendly manner was clearly the result of terrifyingly extensive breeding.

In a way he could have never articulated, he felt sure that she faintly approved of her granddaughter's crush. He wished her goodnight. "And to you, Henry," she said, swanning from the room. "Rebecca," she commanded.

"I will."

They listened to the receding passage of her dress until she reached the carpeted hallway which led to her bedroom.

"'Will' what?" said Henry.

"Do you want to neck?"

"No," he said.

"Yes, you do. But first I'm hungry."

They kissed for a while in the kitchen, Rebecca, up on the counter, legs apart. Later, spooning ice cream out of the carton, she un-suctioned the spoon from her tongue. "What are you smiling about?"

"You," he said. "Oh, to be nine years old again!"

"How old are you?"

"You know this already. Thirty, if I'm a day."

She had turned 21 the month before he met her at a Settlement House benefit he had been bunged into by Bobbie and some mayfly boyfriend of hers. He liked how smart and sparkly she seemed for a girl whose name even *he* knew as a non-reader of the gossip page, but he had nowhere to put her, so to speak, and was stunned by her interest in him.

Saturday morning at the West 100th Street meeting spot the Browns dived into boxes of new uniforms in the trunk of Al's Bonneville. Carloads were reconfigured so that Juan, the catcher, could go over signs with two new pitchers. Henry rode with Eddie Perez, the two Cubans and a Dominican shortstop named Chachi. After missing an exit on I-95, Eddie backed up for a hundred yards.

"Eddie, *cabron*! Are you fucking crazy?"

"Just cool it, man," he said, losing control of his pedal to the floor reverse. "Move your head, I can't see."

"Great," said Henry morosely, noting the Doppler effect of car horns blaring by, "I'm going to die in a Puerto Rican driving cliché."

39

The New Rochelle Robins had a pitcher, shortstop and centerfielder of otherworldly skills. The pitcher was unhittable for the innings he pitched. The shortstop hammered two fastballs so far through sparsely beaded curtains of snow that both homeruns hung in the distance like photographs of balls. Diving headfirst, the centerfielder caught line drives which barely cleared the infield and made a throw on a gapper that detonated in the third baseman's mitt with a sound Henry had never heard on a baseball field. Weeks later when the Browns played the Robins in a real game, these three had embarked on careers in the minor leagues, the centerfielder promoted to the big club when the rosters expanded in September.

"And they ain't the only team up here can play," said Al.

Henry blinked snowflakes off his eyelashes, listened to the wind creaming through his sweatpants, and shivered. The snow stopped in the last inning, and, as they were leaving, the sun came out, but the day became no less cold. Al dropped off the Cubans in Woodlawn and got back on the thruway. Over Manhattan gray cirrus had been replaced with cumuli and the sky was hazy with windblown grit and the fairyland dispersal of tiny white blossoms.

"How's Elizabeth?" Henry asked.

"Went out to California, see her sister."

"She coming back?"

Al shrugged.

The sensation returned to Henry of being suspended in the kind of time measured in half innings. Usually, he felt this way in summer, not spring. I am growing old in joy, he thought. I need to make a change.

Out of the blue Bobbie's friend, Ann, had shown up at his apartment one night. To restore the chubby little monkey of months ago had taken real effort. When she came, rocking against him as before, she seemed pained by the dinginess of his habitat and not at all abandoned to her previous eyeless ecstasy.

"So there's a marble shortage in Philadelphia?"

"Just a sentimental thing," she said. "My Mom. Her old neighborhood."

"Look, I don't have to go to Spanish Harlem with you. You'll probably be safe. A woman up there on her own."

She smiled, wryly aware of being worked.

When they disembarked at 109th Street, the cab went immediately off-duty. In a corner compound guarded by a spiked fence and a rancorous Doberman, Ann and a skinny gnomish Italian sawed back and forth on the merits of various marbles. Finally she made a deposit on a pink slab, polished front and back, its massive edges left raw. For his part, Henry chose not to register the word "inscription."

"My Mom and I, we're real close," said Ann.

"She knew that marble place was still up here."

"DiLello's? She knew. Yeah."

They were now walking home. "Is she sick."

Ann stopped. "Terminal. The marble's her headstone."

"Terminal. Well, what do you know?"

In the glance Ann now shot him Henry saw how his unreadiness for permanent attachment had turned him into a cad. Moments later, snapping her overnight case shut in his apartment, she asked with contempt that he not walk her down.

That Monday Henry reported for work at Fitzgerald Sand & Stone, a ready-mix concrete company operating under a court order and a $10 million judgment which was currently under appeal. Headquartered in Manhattan, Fitzgerald Sand & Stone owned grandfathered-in concrete plants in the Bronx and Harlem. Clearly, Henry could have refused this gig, but Freddy Habyan had advised him to take it. "This is nuts and bolts, short stroke stuff. You love this kind of shit."

"Freddy, the Bronx?"

"What? You miss me, kid?"

Henry stared out the window of the office formerly occupied by Arthur Tannenbaum, who after the Armor Tech debacle had disappeared over the horizon into a Big Eight accounting firm. Apparently Freddy had shared his concerns over the stated figures for the bond issue with Mike Peruwitz, the Division head. This bit of honest eye-rolling had netted him Arthur Tannenbaum's corner office, where Henry now sat sideways in a wing chair. "Ray has me working by myself," he said. "You know what that means."

"Yeah, stealing time for another dumb-ass project of yours. So what? It's a goof off job, anyway. You ever notice this thing Ray has for Irish bars?"

"He's got a new one, but he just goes there to drink."

"Do me a favor, would you? Sit in that chair like a normal person."

Henry stood up. "The atmosphere's getting a little too 'executive' in here." He crossed to the door.

"I'll come up there, have lunch with you. Old times."

"How's your wife?"

"I'm off tits. I'm becoming a leg man."

"Be sure to tell your secretary," Henry said

Freddy's secretary had just entered. "Mr. Habyan," she said with bristly efficiency. "I've rescheduled your appointments."

"See you in the Bronx, sport," said Henry.

Shelves of law books wallpapered Dicko Fitzgerald's office. Dicko's big stony face looked like arrowheads had been chipped out of it. "Some lawyer working for me left 'em behind when he got fired," he said. "Long story short: fucked me over on a hotel bid. Sit down."

On the way over, Ray had said to Henry, "His old man told

him once, 'Richie, I'm gonna buy up every pen in the world so you can't sign your name to anything.' Dicko's a fixer-upper. He'll grab a business, slap it into shape and sell it. He's addicted to incident. It drives his old man nuts."

"Is he guilty?"

"Who knows, but you notice he's not appealing these other charges. Big as he is, he's a bit of a crybaby. It's always somebody else's fault. To Dicko his only knock is he's too nice a guy."

"What am I particularly watching for?"

"The no-shows, the union pay-offs. And of course the price-fixing. If you can figure it out. By the way, that 'reporter' stunt you pulled? You and I need to have a little chat."

"So what do you think?" Dicko asked Henry. "Can you ride herd up there in the Bronx?"

"Sure."

"Henry worked for me at Armor Tech," said Ray.

"I know," said Dicko, snapping a shark-bite out of his sandwich before scouring daintily at the edges of his mouth with a triangle of paper napkin. The garlic stench of deli pickles sustained a vivid presence in the room.

"The suit's without merit. The judgment's onerous, so the verdict's gonna be flipped. You see something not kosher?" he said to Henry. "You come to me. Understand?"

One of the two accountant types at the table tossed down the last of his Dr. Brown's Black Cherry, his nostrils distending as he stifled a burp. "I'm John Merridew. You want, I'll walk you through the General Ledger right now. Show you how we do things here."

"Show away."

Merridew flipped out his tie from the bunchy crease his pants had formed and stood up. He and Henry left the room.

"So how's he gonna do?" Henry heard Dicko ask Ray.

Finally Ray's car service driver found the unmarked exit ramp in the Bronx which debouched from the Bruckner Expressway to the Fitzgerald concrete plant. Mixing silos, loading gantries and conical mountains of fly ash towered over two office trailers. In the days before transit mix trucks concrete manufacture consisted of seven men with shovels and piles of sand, cement and stone. One shovel of cement, two of sand, four of stone. Add water and stir.

In the first trailer a girl raised one pencilled eyebrow at Ray.

Feet on his desk, Henry wore cowboy boots with his suit. Bang! the boots came down from the desk. "Anybody want my roast beef-on-rye. I'm going out to lunch."

"Yeah," someone muttered, "out-to-lunch, all right."

"This may look like a barn, Mr. Birdsall," said an older fierce-looking woman, "but rest assured it is not. Please refrain from shouting like a stevedore."

Outside, the racket of a jackhammer started up. As Ray and Henry passed into the milky April sunlight, the jackhammer noise became painful. Birdsall stopped. "Hear that?"

"You must be joking."

Henry pointed to one of the transit mixers. "Know what that guy's doing?"

"What guy," said Ray, picking up his pace.

"Concrete set up in his drum. He's hammering it out."

"Let's go, Henry. Quick-quick."

"Those trucks cost $150,000. The guy inside there…"

"Tell me inside here." Ray popped into the car.

Henry climbed in front, next to the driver. "Concrete's gotta be poured 90 minutes from when it's mixed, which is why Fitzgerald's such a lock. They're the only ones close enough to Manhattan. You see these drivers lined up at sites, hosing the drums down? That's why. To keep the concrete from setting."

"How does the poor guy keep his hearing?"

"And listen to this. He's an ex-cop, the one in the drum. He quits the NYPD to work for Uncle Dicko. Third day on the job, *this* happens. Where we headed?"

"Out of the Bronx. Or would you prefer eating here?"

Home early enough that night for dinner with Dora and the girls, Ray relayed to his wife the parts of his conversation with Henry Birdsall he thought she might enjoy. The Rebecca Van Rijn parts. "This man works for you? Girls, stop that!"

"Can we go outside?" said Melissa. "We're finished."

"You may go when you're excused. Is he a blueblood or something?"

"I don't think he is, no."

"Did you meet her?"

"I told you I did."

"But, Ray, I don't understand. You have people working for you that someone like her would be interested in? All right, you're excused," she said. The girls hopped off their chairs and raced out of the room.

"He's from near Philadelphia. What's that called, the Main Line? One of my spear carriers for Armor Tech."

"Ray, you promised."

"Dora, they're not even in the room."

She lowered her voice. "Karen asked me yesterday. She saw a headline in the paper. 'Didn't Daddy have something to do with that?'"

"You know what," said Ray proudly. "I think she's going to be a businessman, woman, businesswoman, whatever. I met the mother once. I ever tell you that?"

"At a rally to save Grand Central. Yes, you did. And that she was stranger looking than she was in the papers, but with a magnetism. That's what you said, a 'magnetism.'"

"The daughter doesn't really look like her."

"She's very young, isn't she?"

"They don't seem to fit, Birdsall and her. He told me it's exhausting, going out with someone so young."

"I left the lease out for you."

"And you like the place?"

She shrugged. "For a summer rental."

That afternoon at a rathskellar on Second Avenue Ray had flushed out of Birdsall details of the case against Armor Tech.

"Transcripts," said Henry. "That's all she gave me."

"Nothing about stock fraud?"

"Does this whole case swing on the stocks being valued at insider prices or is any payment in stock illegal?" Henry probed at his weisswurst. "The operative meat in here is veal, right?"

"So you thought you were going to be indicted?"

"No, but people further up the birth canal, I did."

"Would you have tipped me off?"

"You know what? Probably I would have."

"And then done what? Turned States?

"As a *Times* reporter?"

Ray laughed. "Right."

"I would have known what was coming."

"I'm going to pass on to you the benefit of my knowledge. Let me rephrase that," Ray said when Henry gave him a mocking cross-eyed look. "We can keep each other informed. I, personally, took no Armor Tech stock as either payment or gift. Did I ramrod the comfort letter through? Yes. But forget about that. What we *do* have to worry about are stock payments to the firm we weren't aware of. To answer your question, any payment in stock for services rendered is illegal."

"Gotcha."

Jesus, Ray thought, this kid really does annoy me. And then he realized Henry was trying to annoy him. And Henry, seeing Ray see this, laughed.

In his political career, a wave of good will had lifted Al high enough to see the far shore. After an approach by a State Assemblyman who wanted him to run for a seat on the City Council, he called Elizabeth in California. "What's it like out there?"

"I could get used to this," she said.

Because she professed an interest, Al kept her abreast of his political news. At times, she seemed still to be coordinating his actions. Certainly, he missed her. Gradually he began to "see" her in the kitchen or lying flat on her face on his fold-out bed. He had not expected this. Her image should have faded, not grown more present.

In the late spring baseball parachutists dropped out of the sky, college players whose seasons had ended, ex-minor leaguers looking for a team. Al had one walk-on who insisted he had spent spring training in Florida with the Baltimore Orioles, a tall wide black kid driving an expensive car and carrying specially made Louisville sluggers in an Oriole equipment bag.

"Al, who the fuck is this?" Birdsall asked.

"Frank Robinson, probably."

On the phone, the kid had listed the Oriole farm system as his bona fides. And now, fully uniformed in Baltimore home whites, he click-clacked in his spikes across the concrete parking lot, his sunshades flipped down under his Oriole's cap.

"Bill Baker," he said. "Here to play."

"Play what?"

In the moment it took for the large serious face of Bill Baker to register the fact that he was being hazed, Al regretted living in a world where wishing for a thing could not make it so. "I'll play in this uniform 'til you see what I can do."

"And when'll that be?"

"Let me get loose."

Portentously, the young man set down his equipment bag on the dugout bench. Took out his mitt, its leather gleaming with expensiveness. Took out his self-autographed bats, placing the handle-rounds exactly in the chain link openings of the fence. Took out his supple new batting gloves, flapping the fingers artistically out of the back pocket of his uniform pants. Removed his Oriole's warm-up jacket from his equipment bag and from the jacket drew a packet of tobacco chaw-style bubblegum and crammed a wad into his mouth. Carried the warm-up jacket carefully out to the grass near the foul line and laid the jacket on the grass, arms out. Smacked a brand new baseball into his mitt and looked around finally for a throwing partner.

"Boog Powell there needs somebody," Al said to Henry.

Birdsall grimaced, yelled over to the kid. Wagged a warm-up ball, "Use this one." Then fired the ball to Bill Baker, who was so tenderly glancing at his own new ball that only an ungainly mitt-flap allowed him to catch the one thrown at him.

"Who's that," asked Spider Givens, an outfielder who had played A Ball with the Mets. "He miss their team bus or something?" Bill Baker's first throw had sailed about eight feet over Birdall's head.

"Sorry, man. Gotta get my distance down."

Birdsy jogged down the rightfield line to retrieve, and fired a screamer back, which broke sharply, ticking off the tip of Bill Baker's giant outfield mitt. From then on Bill played catch with elaborate care and small velocity.

"Ask Boog, what his position is."

"First base and the outfield," Birdsall called back.

Hearing this, Bill Baker's face lit up in hopes of playing today. "Maybe he can pinch hit," conceded Al.

A girl in the stands periodically razzed Birdsall in what sounded to Al like a cultured voice. She looked familiar, too. Birdsy, who had arrived with this individual in a dusty red Fiat, was not above dating a TV actress.

"You driving now?"

"She wouldn't have fit in your piece of shit."

48

"Actually, he was embarrassed," said the girl.

"I bet he was," said Al.

When Birdsall introduced her, Al immediately forgot her name. Cute, not actress cute, but fresh-looking, and Birdsy seemed proud of her, although he acted proud of every girl he brought to watch him play. "What you looking for, anyway?" Al asked him once. "My parental consent."

Birdsall laughed and said, not quite kidding, "Yeah."

In weak sunlight which gradually turned whitish, the Browns played the Pelham Mets. The Browns won the first game 8-0 on a shutout thrown by a kid who in another week was to report to a low level affiliate of the Minnesota Twins. Eddie Perez pitched the second game and got hammered, 14-3. When the Dominican shortstop vanished after the first game, Sonny Suarez successfully lobbied Al for his old position back. By the third inning Sonny had committed four errors.

After the game, Al assembled his remaining multitude. "I am sick and tired of these black and Hispanic mistakes. I don't mind we get our brains beat in legit, but either fucking concentrate, or play somewheres else."

Bill Baker, who struck out, looking feeble, in his one at bat, came up afterwards to Al. "Think I can get me a uniform?"

In no mood for this Al said, "Stay dressed like you are."

"My timing's off is all."

Al relented. "Schedule's in my bag."

Later that night, he went downstairs by himself to the Adage Lounge. Times like these he especially missed Elizabeth. Sunday night and not too many regulars around. His dogs missed Elizabeth, too. He was the one who fed and walked them, but if they did not feel up to par they went to her, and she wasn't even a dog lover. "What you looking at?" she would say to Al, the beagle. "Oh, all right." Down she would bend to him with a food scrap, or to fondle his dewlaps. "Not too much different from you," she would say to Al.

"Play today?" asked the bartender, Mike.

"Yeah. Shot and a beer, I'm good to go."

"Nothing here, that's for sure."

"Not looking."

Why was it she would not come back? Because the comfort of habit could also trap: he saw that now. The new did not manifest itself quickly enough when you had grown up pretty much where you still lived. Elizabeth had no interest in being contextualized. That was an aspiration she had ascribed to Al. Al Scoville, Man of the People, Al of Upper Broadway. Truly, he realized, she had wanted all along to be Elizabeth of Somewhere Else.

"Tired tonight," he said to Mike, who shrugged.

Rebecca greeted the doorman, Link, and the elevator man, Gridley, and then Harriet, who told her she had gotten too much sun. Dutifully, she ducked into grandmother's room, who ate her dinner there so she could watch a PBS special on that TV because she liked its picture better. Grandfather Livingston looked up from his legal papers as she passed the library door on her way back out an hour later. "Going somewhere?"

"You mean with who? Henry."

"Have fun. Not too late now."

"You met him."

"That's nice," he said, and went back to his papers.

Walking up Park, she felt electrically charged. I am going to meet my lover, she thought to herself, and then smiled at her own silliness. As she pushed through the restaurant door, she could sense heads turning, the doubletakes. She spotted Henry at the bar. He greeted her, acting like she was any other girl. His looseness encouraged teasing and the teasing made her more like a sister than a date, which relaxed them both.

"Do you bring all your girlfriends here?"

"Almost all," he said.

"Will they be upset?"

"They'll work through it."

"So what eating club were you in at Princeton?"

"Ivy. Are you out of college yet?"

"Is that a good one?"

"Yes, it is. Let's talk about your report card."

From other tables she could feel glances, the heightened sense of presence she brought to a room. Although she had had serious boyfriends in prep school and college and had not been a virgin for about a year, this was her first grownup romantic moment in New York. Not a crush or the heart-race of first love, but a slower, warmer sensation she was beginning to think she liked better.

For Rebecca the life of this Henry Birdsall person went off in unexpected directions. For instance, that Irish bar he had taken her to and the government lawyer he had tricked and his appalled boss and that arms factory in the Bronx constantly in the papers. "Sometimes the best people get scared off," she told him. "They're afraid of looking like they want to meet you. Whereas, the ones you don't want..."

"What do you mean?"

"Because of. You know."

"Oh, right."

"They're the ones pursuing you."

He shrugged. "Makes sense, I guess."

What she wanted to say was, "I never meet people like you," but knew that was a bad idea and then said it anyway. She was able, though, when he made a wry face, to keep her other feelings to herself.

Down Sunday-night-empty Park Avenue he escorted her back to her apartment. "They're asleep," she whispered as they tread softly through the foyer. A light burned in the library. She turned to him, knowing he was nervous.

"Really," she said, "they're in bed."

But it was pretty inescapable what had to happen next. She threw herself down on the couch and without a word they began to neck. She squirmed around so she could get one of her breasts against his chest and he cupped the ridge of her hip and then ran his hand across her bottom. Probably afraid of being walked in on, he did not feel her up. She rolled against him, touching his stiffness with her upper leg.

"Let's go to my room," she said.

He nodded. Trying not to see this moment as historic, she led him down the hallway to her bedroom.

Her lack of experience must have seemed obvious to him because he acted the gentleman. He did not just pull up her skirt and yank down her panties, rubbing at her with one hand before sticking himself in. No, he undid his shirt, button by button, while she unwound her skirt. She hesitated at her panties, then turned off the bedside light. He pulled off his pants and she got one quick glimpse of the rod nudging the waist elastic of his boxers. He pulled the covers back and she removed her blouse and bra. In she slid under the duvet and he slid in next to her, and on their backs under the covers they writhed off panties and underwear. A few days later she would find hers with her foot, bringing back mixed but, on balance, exciting memories.

She tried to be active, if that was the word. He massaged her breasts, but seemed somewhat in a hurry. She was wet. She knew that was never a problem. She got one glimpse of his redness and length, and then, wow, he was in her.

"Does that feel good," she asked, not quite sure if it did.

"Yes. Just keep doing that."

"What am I doing?"

"Here." He got his hands under her bottom and began pushing at her. Obediently, she pushed back.

And then she remembered kissing. She took his face in her hands, which was dark and preoccupied, and began to kiss him on the lips, which felt much more important than what was happening below, beneath, inside. She pushed her tongue into his mouth, and he began grappling at her breasts, all the time moving, and she could feel his nipples harden, and then he seemed to be rising inside her and jerking and she felt a wetness running out of her, which she knew was his. She lay there thinking she was exhausted, but knew she was not, and yet was happy to have this over with. They had started at last.

"Ooops, wait!" She slid out from under him, imagining a yellow stain on the mattress cover and the maid showing it to Harriet. Later, he knocked on the bathroom door and came in. She had cleaned herself out and had her nightgown in hand.

"Do you want to wash off?"

"Sure," he said.

"You're trying to make me feel relaxed, aren't you?"

"Why not," he said. But that was what he was doing.

"Will you tuck me in?"

He laughed. But leaning over her bed, he kissed her goodnight. Warm in her nightgown, with some of him still running down her thigh, she felt cozy and adult and, more importantly, safe with him and happy, very happy right now.

Before she fell asleep, she envisioned him tiptoeing down the hallway, letting himself out the front door, exhaling softly while he waited for the night man to take him down. While he was getting dressed, she caught him glancing above her bed at the framed photographs of her mother and father, and those of her famous relatives. He shook his head and looked back at her. She grinned. He took a deep breath and raised his eyebrows, changing the subject, so to speak. But she had never felt more like a princess.

The Colonial League had no games Mother's Day weekend, so Henry lacked a legitimate excuse when Buster called. "Your mother wants to talk to you about Bobbie. I don't want to sound mysterious, but she'd rather not do it over the phone."

"How about Mother's Day."

"You're kidding! You mean there's an actual day set aside for mothers? Who the hell came up with that idea? By the way, don't forget Father's Day."

Years before, after Henry and Bobbie had whined that Buster never asked any of his children what they were doing, and had shuddered over his answer, "I'm afraid to hear," Buster had gone through a grisly period of asking personal questions of his offspring and feigning interest in the answers. Henry had begged him to stop, but Bobbie continued to test Buster's resolve by forcing him to listen to endless *inscripta* of personal trauma, most of which were made up.

"You don't really, do you?"

"What, make them up? Of course I do. He needs it. And so does Gwenny. Either they're either over-involved in our lives or else they're trapped in their own little thought bubbles. It's called 'projective narcissism.'"

"Did you make that up, too?"

"So she told you she wants to talk to you about me."

Henry and Bobbie lay by the pool, Bobbie, fully dressed and sweating, Henry, in his bathing trunks. "How about a cheat sheet?" he said. "You know, key phrases underlined in red."

"I'm getting married again."

"Well, try not to act so excited."

"I'm not really," she said, missing his sarcasm.

"Did I ever tell you what I think about you and them?"

"No, and this would be a good time not to."

"Two summers ago, when you got married again, I said to you and Theodore, maybe even in front of whatever girl I was down here with, God, I'm trying to think who that was, but you probably don't remember, do you, that I'd get married in three years, very specific about the number. "

"Fuck it," said Bobbie, standing up. "Are you trying to bore me to death, or just do a really long sentence without using a verb? Yeah, I remember. So what?"

"It's two years and counting."

"So get married, you fag."

"See? I deflected your self-pity. What's his name?"

"I'm too depressed. Ask Guinivere."

Bobbie then vanished up the path to the house and Henry closed his eyes. His compliance job with Fitzgerald Sand & Stone had curled up at the edges. Trying to pin down Liability figures in the General Ledger, he kept bumping up against suspicious entries for Wages Paid.

"You got pay stubs, W2's? There's all kinds of names here I can't put faces to."

Karen Mulroney stared at him. "The W2's go to Dicko, once we journal them. You've seen those, haven't you, the journals?" She phrased the question like a taunt.

"Karen, do you know where I used to work?"

"Why. Would I possibly care. Where you used to work."

Those who overheard Henry's attempt at a power play knew he had consulted at Armor Tech and what he meant by bringing that up. The face of office manager, Rollo McIntyre, already unhealthily pale, turned even paler.

"Twenty full-time employees," Henry continued, "except I only see twelve at a time. Can somebody sit with me, go through these personnel records?"

"I suggest, Mr. Birdsall," responded Rollo, "that you trot around introducing yourself to each of our hard-working men and women and ask them their names and hours."

One of the roughnecks entered from the other trailer, Dicko's nephew, Frank, a blue-eyed, black-haired Celt. "Looks like someone's getting their balls broke," he said.

"Mr. Birdsall, here," said Karen, "is implying we've got ghosts working for us. What would you think of that, now?"

"Payroll padders, is it?" said Frank.

"I just need some fucking figures."

"Doing your job then, are you? Your life's calling."

Remembering his shame at being mocked, Henry felt his chest grow tight. "There you are," said his mother. She sat down on the recliner. "Did you talk with Bobbie?"

"Who's the guy?"

"I think she's going to back out."

He stared at her.

"Henry, tell me what you're doing up there, please?"

"In New York? New girlfriend, I think."

She leaned forward and in her sudden avidity he realized what a mistake he had made. As though imagining her own triumph she proceeded to relieve him of every detail relevant to his potential entry into the Van Rijn family.

"I'm only going out with her, for Christ's sake," he insisted when Buster loomed up beside him in a crimson irrepressible joy. "She's a child!"

"Your mother was 21 when I married her."

"And very immature, I might add," added Guinivere.

"You guys should be doing what you do to me," said Bobbie. "You know, where you try not to act too excited when I stumble on someone you approve of." She turned to Henry. "Actually, younger makes sense for you."

"Young for my age, etcetera. But I'm not really, am I?

"What? Immature?" Bobbie patted his hand, which he immediately snatched away. "Of course not, little man."

On the Sunday afternoon of Mother's Day, he stood beside his car with his sister, trying to decide whether the shrinkage he had noticed in her psyche resulted from his leapfrog over her in his parents' estimation. "You upset?"

"I don't know what I am," she said. "Got any ideas?"

"About how you should feel? Like me, I guess. Out there making no headway, but no one caring much either… Shit, now *I'm* in the golden chair!"

She laughed. "Lucky little man."

"We've been over this before. Lucky large man, thank you very much."

His parents, which they never normally did, came out to say goodbye.

S arah Mortensen had cancelled two meetings with the reporter-imposter, Henry Birdsall, since running into him with Ray Levin. She had even seen Ray at Dean's in the interim when she brought along her paralegal, Candy Geren, a sweet girl from the Midwest who at Shea, Gould called herself Candace. A soft white-skinned blonde, Candy was a little chubby on the curves, but cool along the centerboard and smart. Sarah liked her.

"Shame we don't have any of our Lotharios around," said Ray. Candy glanced at the crowd, not at all disappointed in the absence of passable men.

"How's your stool pigeon doing," said Sarah. "The one with the fancy girlfriend?"

"You ever spank him?"

"It's all in the anticipation, Ray."

On the promenade, unobserved, Sarah now watched Henry expectorate into the sliding slate of the East River current. She checked her new Cartier watch, a slender gold band which made her feel slender and golden, too. A half hour remained before her dinner party. Myron Kandel, a Shea Gould senior partner, and his wife, Eve, were having a few people in. A little late would be good, Sarah reflected. Already around the firm she had become Sarah The Character: brilliant, slightly eccentric, the bride of corporate law.

"Want to sit?" Henry asked. "A little windy out here."

Sarah eyed the green depths of Carl Shurz Park, its street lamps an hour shy of illuminating themselves. "I don't mind a breeze. Besides, two murders here the last six months."

"The Decepticons. Gang stuff. Killing people with golf clubs," said Henry eagerly.

When the river wind moulded her frock to her figure, she caught Henry's eye traveling to her bust. Forced to wonder how she looked, she was annoyed. "You won't get off the hook talking to me," she said. "If the tide starts running against them, they'll bring tampering charges and you'll be in the dock. So let me ask you again. Did you pass on the material I gave you to anyone?"

"I should have fucking destroyed it. No, I did not."

"Did you discuss what was in it with anyone?"

"I told Ray what you gave me. And that there was nothing in there about stock fraud."

"Let's sit down."

As they repaired to the benches through an enfilade of joggers, Sarah weighed the option of plating herself up with legal armor. Case law references ran through her mind, but then she remembered her vow to live the unhemmed-in life of consequence-be-damned.

"Can I ask you a question?" he said. "Off the record?"

"That's pretty funny, coming from you."

"In your former career as a prosecutor…"

"What's the question?"

"Cash in a briefcase. Which I wasn't supposed to see."

She looked at her watch. "Exactly how naïve are you?"

"The problem is, a little too sophisticated. I figured it was union payoffs. Now, I'm not so sure."

"What am I supposed to do with this information?"

"Think about it and tell me what I saw." Sensitive to her watch consultation, he stood up. "I'll walk you out. No sense some thug playing 'Fore' with your forehead."

They headed down East End Avenue. "Dinner party?" he asked. When Sarah nodded, he said, "I'll get you a cab." But, for the moment, they kept walking.

"This dinner I'm going to?" she said, "the host handles the Van Rijn estate. Also her grandparents' affairs."

"Listen," he said, "I'm consulting for a concrete company appealing a judgment. I don't know why I'm telling you this, but when concrete sets up in one of those transit mixers, it has to be jackhammered out. I'm there close to a month and the guy's still working."

"There's a cab."

"I'll grab him," he said, but the cab kept going.

"You were saying." She glanced again at her watch.

"You let stuff seize up inside of you? You have to jack-hammer it out. I should have followed up on that briefcase thing. Here's one." A cab banged to a stop.

Myron Kandel's apartment on Sutton Place sat high enough over the East River to reduce to a whisper the buffet of traffic on the FDR Drive. Quite pleasant, thought Sarah, at an balcony window clutching a flute of champagne. Construction workers then clanged a grappling hook into a boat on the water. The sound could be heard as though ten feet away.

Later, at dinner, she asked the table, "How would you like to have to jackhammer out any mistake you made."

"Apropos of?" asked Myron.

"If concrete hardens in one of those revolving drums?"

"Those big trucks always holding up traffic?"

"It has to be jackhammered out."

"Really," said a Deputy Mayor.

"And like my father used to say," said an industrialist. "'Concrete is for keeps.'"

"Harry's father was a developer in Queens."

"Not *that* Queens developer," said Harry, laughing.

"Thank God!" said Eve Kandel.

LaChaix, the investment banker, leaned forward. "He's going to lose his shirt with those casinos." Which was when Sarah realized they were talking about Donald Trump.

In the living room after dinner, a portly European rainmaker for Paul, Weiss asked Sarah, "Who is it you know in the concrete business?" Bushy gray hair wreathed his dome like a laurel. He also affected a watch chain. "Myron was telling me you were a prosecutor for Bob Abrams."

Sarah smiled. "Who are you representing?"

"At this point, purely advisory. Tell your friend the best way to stay out of concrete, in terms of footwear, is to keep your eye unpeeled and your ear closed."

"I will," said Sarah. She could have run down the

defendant list and guessed who the man was "advising," but did not wish to consider this a preliminary hunt for a back channel into the Armor Tech prosecution team.

She met Candy for a late drink at an actor hangout on Columbus Avenue. Eventually, Candy stopped trying to magnetize notice from surly, stubbly-bearded Prince Charmings. Stopped trying to be picked up. Started calibrating potential damage to her self-esteem, which was never so endangered as Candy imagined it was. Started to enjoy herself. With Sarah.

Afterwards she came up to Sarah's apartment. "I'm going to have a headache tomorrow," she promised, staring around the living room, impressed.

Sarah showed her the bedroom, the eat-in-kitchen, the tiny dining room. And then announced she was buying a co-op in the Beresford, just around the corner.

"You're kidding! But this is so nice."

"Well," Sarah admitted, "I'm thinking about it, anyway. I just made an offer. On a two bedroom."

Feeling she needed a draft of air, she walked Candy to her subway stop. They hugged goodnight. "A two bedroom," said Candy, a note in her voice of Sarah could not tell what. Of what she hoped for, she hoped, as Candy angled unsurely down the subway steps.

"Figure it out," said Dicko to Henry in a Chinese restaurant.

"You got people on payroll who don't actually have to be there, you mean. Unless you need extra crew."

"Margins are fixed so you've got the luxury to run it loose. We're big, but we're still Mom and Pop." Dicko snapped his fingers for the check. "You never met Hughie Lynch?"

"Frankie and John are his kids?"

"Jack, not John. See, this is what I'm talking about. Hughie's my cousin. Tipped me off when Sand & Stone was in play. Now his kids are working for me and Hughie runs one of my companies." Standing, Dicko was the size of a polar bear. Onto the table he chipped a lettuce of $20 bills.

"The thing is," said Henry as they waded up Lexington. "Some of these folks on payroll, they're way too old to work."

"Welfare, you heard of that? Mostly they were with the guy, Casey, I took the company off of. I inherited 'em. Here," he said, "take my watch. I'll say it's for Murder when I go in."

"Go in?"

"That way nobody'll bother me. You sending me to jail, right? So I gotta take off my watch." The watch that Dicko refastened, chuckling, as they rode the elevator.

"Just remember, kid, we're not making bond issues here. Hughie? You know this guy?"

In his office Hugh Lynch looked up from a triple decker checkbook. "This guy? No, but I can guess." Gray eyes, magnified by glasses, ears large enough to hinge, Hugh Lynch resembled the Catholic cardinal, O'Connor. "Henry, is it? Hope you're finding everything to your liking up there. Frankie says you've made quite a stir."

"He's keeping us honest, Hugh."

"Good lad!"

"Your son, Frank, was quite a help," said Henry. "Which reminds me, who's Pete McCann related to?"

"The former policeman? Dicko'll tell you."

While Dicko quick-scanned memos at his desk, Henry glanced at the framed photographs of Dicko's wife, a lovely blonde, and his two children. "Sit over here on the couch. No, closer. I wanna tell you something. The one-ten in Queens, the stationhouse? You know the place, the problems they had?"

"Shakedowns?" Henry guessed.

"Pete McCann," said Dicko. "And now he's with us."

"A fucking Ahab," said Henry. "Stabbing that whale with a jackhammer."

Dicko laughed. "Ahab. That's pretty good."

"Out of curiosity, how many companies do you own?"

"Before this lawsuit? Eight. My old man's old man was a coal miner. My old man made his pile in bricks. I got brothers, they work for companies, they don't own 'em. He worries about me, my Dad, but I give him a kick. He's like, 'what the hell's he gonna do next?'"

"Is Water Tunnel one of your companies?"

"Fuck these City pricks, by the way. The suit's bullshit."

"Reason I ask about Water Tunnel is, apart from what does it do, which I have no idea. I have my own little water thing going. A floating parking garage."

Dicko had absorbed himself in a legal letter. With a small groan of satisfaction he tossed the letter across his desk. Ears flaming at having humiliated himself, Henry skimmed it.

"Cocksucker I fired," said Dicko. "Took three million in judgments off his back. See how I'm getting repaid?"

"What's a *lis pendens*?"

"Clouds title on the properties. Lenders, buyers. This is the kind of shit I wade in every day!" Dicko sighed. Eyed his telephone longingly. Henry stood up. "Floating garage? What the hell," said Dicko. "Why not?"

"Just the coincidence. You know, 'water?' Listen. I found no-shows on the rolls. You gotta fix that."

"Send me the names, we'll stop the checks."

In his office, Hugh Lynch, still at his check-writing labors, rested his large hands over the triple decker, innocence beaming out of his homely face. "Water Tunnel?" Henry asked. "Are those Water Tunnel checks?"

"That they are," said Hugh.

"Because we see quite a few as Sand & Stone deposits."

"Cash reserve," said Hugh, reverently. "We're building it up from profits elsewhere. The hotel, for instance."

"Your accounts have been emptied by the bond?"

"Exactly."

For weeks now, Henry had slighted his entrepreneurial ambitions. To escape the claustral boredom of wading through time tickets up in the Bronx he would slip into the workyard to watch concrete being mixed. Watch Pete McCann, working on his drum. "Did you like being a cop?"

"It was alright. Make more money doing this."

"Really."

"Yes, really. What you think a rookie pulls down?"

Pete slumped on a concrete chunk, dust-white jackhammer beside him. A sadness prevailed here, the sadness of being Irish. Trucks arrived and departed, invoices got paid, people talked on the phone and went home. Night fell. All along the city shoreline skeletons footed in blocks of New York concrete waved like kelp in the underwater currents.

"What about working for Dicko?"

"It's a living. Way to support my family. You married?"

"No."

But Henry now saw what separated him from these people. They belonged to each other and to the lives they led. As he realized this, swimming into his vision came the image of himself in his apartment, working on his prospectus. Out of this niggling, he realized, would emerge the person he really was.

"I like him for you," said Diana. "For now."

"Yes, but why do *you* like him?" said Laura, her daughter.

"Because he's. Different," Rebecca said.

"He doesn't seem very different to me."

They sat on the brick side terrace of her Aunt Diana's house in Southhampton. Rebecca adjusted her swimsuit top.

"Are you getting busty?" Diana asked.

"I bet he went to prep school," said Laura.

"Then guess how come he didn't drive out last night? Because he has a baseball game. And he works in the Bronx. He does real things. He's not going right into the... I don't know what, the upper echelons."

"The '*upper echelons*?'" said her cousin, laughing.

"What does Priscilla think?" said Diana. "More to the point, I wonder what Georgina would have thought."

"Grandmother likes him. Mother would've, too."

"So did I," Laura said, "the one time I met him." With satisfaction, Rebecca noted the annoyance in Laura's voice, as though one time was not enough.

"When will he be here? Eunice," Diana called through the french doors to a passing maid, "tell Patty, more ice tea."

"Yes, Mrs. Livingston."

Rebecca stretched, happily. Her wet hair felt stiff on her shoulders. She would wash it and be all fresh-smelling when he arrived. "'Becca's in love," sing-songed Laura.

"For dinner, right?" said her Aunt. "And when are the cousins coming? He's here for dinner, right, Rebecca?"

"Yes, Diana, he's here for dinner."

"Well, he's a good-looking boy," she said.

"Thank you," said Rebecca, smirking at Laura.

As she came downstairs later, wondering if she had been

too active with the makeup brush, Rebecca discovered that she was nervous over the impression Henry might make. He had met Alex, Laura's brother, and Jenny and Nick, but not Rex, Tony and Miranda, nor Aunt Millicent and Uncle George.

Tony's black Porsche ghosted into the driveway.

"So who's this new boyfriend I keep hearing about?" he asked. Which was exactly when Henry arrived. Climbing out of his car, he grinned at Rebecca, who felt proud of him, yes, and also a tiny bit relieved that he had changed clothes and not just driven out here in his baseball suit.

"Nice to meet you, Henry" said Millicent, her youngest aunt before everyone went in to dinner. Rebecca found this hard to believe, but when Henry smiled, Millie blushed.

"They're talking about you," Rebecca noted later. "Diana just smiled at me. I guess you made the grade."

Irritation flickered across Henry's face. To her surprise he did not seem to care whether he was accepted by her tribe. She then glanced around the room trying to see her family through his eyes. The dominant genetic types ran to stubby blondes and tall Ichabod Cranes. All had large teeth, prominent noses, good chins and light-colored eyes. In Dutch fashion, practicality and accessibility marked the sexuality of family females. As per the English, the men were rotters, driven more by joy of conquest than joy of sex. Or so her mother had once remarked.

Once dinner concluded, Henry and Rebecca were left alone with Diana and Uncle George. "A platform into," Henry said, "right. Probably something of my own."

"So a start up. What kind of business experience?"

Because they sat on the couch together, thighs touching, Rebecca could actually feel Henry bridle. "What about your floating thing?" she said. She had once heard him mention something about parking cars on a boat.

"An MBA from NYU. Four years at Cross & Case. Six different consulting engagements, running from…"

"That's fine," said George. "I was only curious."

"We could find Jenny and Rex," Rebecca said, once they had fled. "Or there'll be some of them at the Willman's."

"Your cousins? Whatever you want?"

"Aren't you kind of up to here with cousins?"

"They're okay," he said, "so far."

On a small patio by the gardner's shed they found Rex, Miranda and Jenny snorting coke from a mirror. "Just give me one," said Rebecca. Doing her line, she then held up the mirror to Henry. "You don't have to if you're in training."

He laughed. Indicated the last line on the mirror to Jenny, who shrugged. Henry snorted it.

"In training for what?" said Miranda.

At the Willman's, big Annette, Annette's mother, came downstairs hours later and told them all to go home, although she insisted on being introduced to Henry. "I sympathize," he said to her, which made Rebecca feel stupid and young.

On the way back to the Livingston's, Rebecca pulled Henry aside to neck. He seemed a little bored until she told him Aunt Diana had insomnia and checked who slept in which bed. He stared at the gardener's shed. She did, too.

"That, I never thought of," she said.

"Is it locked?"

No. So they went inside. "Is there a light?" No, but in the darkness the stink of potting soil and insecticide definitely oppressed. "Christ!" he said. But he was driven with the idea.

"We can make a *little* noise in the house," she said.

"There's a shelf over there. Can you lean against it?"

"You mean. How?"

"Here. We've got some moonlight. Goddamnit," he said, "what's this, ant killer?" She had backed up against the shelf and was kissing him. "Can you? Shit, I'm too tall. Kind of sit. Is there enough room?"

"I think so."

Then he began to laugh, and so did she.

"Hurry up," he said moments later, climbing naked into her bed. It waved at her as he straddled her to pull her jersey off, and then he flopped down on top of her and she was barely wet when he went inside. Afraid Laura would come in, she kept looking past his shoulder. "I locked the door," he said.

She found that unlikely, but she forgot about Laura, until the bed began to squeak. "Okay, try this," he said, and flipped her over, impaling her on top of him. She pushed at him, hands on his chest. She felt something new, not much, but something, and then he came. She fell on him and kissed him. Fuck Laura! she could come in now. They both fell asleep, however, and Laura did come in, drunk, waking them up.

"Just let me go into the bathroom," she said.

Rebecca was stunned not to be embarrassed. She heard faucet sounds and the toilet flushing, but by then Henry had kissed her goodnight, tucked himself into his pants and tiptoed, shirtless, into the hall. Laura came out in her nightie and dropped onto her bed. Looked at Rebecca with one eye, the other pressed into the pillow. "I don't care," she said.

"Neither do I."

Henry lay in bed the next morning, euphoric. Alex emerged from the bathroom dressed in topsiders and a polo shirt. "Your turn," he said, delighted to have another male face in the weekend mix.

"Why no shorts?" said Rebecca in the dining room.

"Or your baseball uniform," said Laura.

"Women and children present," he said. "No shorts."

"He has birdlegs," said Rebecca with authority.

Diana tapped out her cigarette and stood up. "Do you play tennis, Henry?"

"Only under duress."

"Hear that?" said Diana to Millie, who had just entered the room. "Get Nicky and we've got doubles."

"No, you don't!" said Rebecca. "He's playing with me."

In a pair of borrowed shorts Henry struggled to recall muscle memories from childhood tennis lessons. Gradually, the pacing and ground strokes came back to him, but keeping his shots within the lines was another matter. "Why don't you just hit it *over* the fence," said Diana, struggling to free one of his line-drives from the chain link webbing.

"He can hit it into the ocean," said Rebecca proudly.

The two aunts played well, understanding, as Henry did not, the geometry of the game. Highly competitive, Rebecca was an athlete, but a slacker in the pursuit of well-placed shots.

"You're pretty fucking good," Henry said.

"You're not."

"Yeah, but I'm frightening them."

"Quit flirting, you two," Millie called across the net.

Cousins had drifted down to the court to assess Henry's character as revealed in the template of sports. Subliminally, he noted body types of the female cousins. In shorts and bathing suit tops they tended towards a boxy healthiness. Veiny and muscular, the male cousins appeared self-cherishing and class conscious. After the softball game, Henry floated on his laurels in the swimming pool. Batting opposite-handed, he had smacked two homeruns over the privet hedges.

"Here," said Rebecca. The others had gone inside for lunch. At the deep end, his hands around her waist, they stayed afloat by synchronized foot-kicking, upper leg to groin. She reached out behind him, took hold of the concrete pool lip. He could feel her nipples engorge against his chest.

"Why are you doing this? You know what's going to happen." Eyes closed, she smiled. "It's embarrassing: sperm floating in the water. She was using him to shock her family, struggling against her own self-perception as demure.

"Lunch, 'Becca," called Eunice, the maid.

Rebecca went streaming up the pool ladder, grabbing his towel, too. "Come on," Henry pleaded.

"No, not until you're ready. And, remember, we can see you from the dining room." Taunting him with a silly little butt wiggle, she padded wet-footed into the house.

With Rebecca and a selection of cousins, Henry went to a movie that night. Rex, the craziest of the Van Rijn's, turned out to be a graduate of Harvard Med. Tony, a Livingston, had an M.A. in Political Science from Yale and worked for the Ford Foundation. Joining them was a Harvard friend of Rebecca's, Alan Green, an editor at the *New York Times Magazine*, along with his girlfriend, Amy, a reporter for the Metro page.

"Did you tell them about your career in newspapers?"

"You worked for the *Times*?" asked Amy.

"In a manner of speaking."

"He likes to tell people that," Rebecca said. "As a joke. He thinks it's funny."

"Well, it is funny, if it isn't true."

Rebecca would be staying the week in Southhampton, so Henry drove back to the city for an assessment at the Harlem River plant. Dicko had actually removed a few no-shows from the payroll. At the Bronx facility faces Henry had never seen before except as names attached to checks showed up to introduce themselves. These included several older females in purchasing, the widows of former employees, who swore they worked from home. "Okay, that's fine. I'm not talking about these kind of people," Henry told Karen Mulroney, who was tormenting him now with hyper-attention to payroll matters.

"But why?" he said that night to Frank Lynch.

"Stancik, the district guy? Dues, what do you think?"

"But cash? Why not a check?"

"What can I tell you. It's how it's done."

Henry and the two Lynch brothers, black-Irish Frank, and Jack, were drinking in an Irish bar in Woodside. Jackie was redhaired and heavily freckled, his eyes a disquieting gray.

"Goddamnit!" Henry said. "Cash in a briefcase again."

"Dues comes out the paychecks. Five unions we're dealing with," said Frank. "You know that."

"We get struck constantly," said Jackie.

"Next time get a receipt and ask the guy, 'Can I look in the bag.'" Frank laughed. "Yeah, he'll be pleased with that."

Near the jukebox a table of fluffy-haired girls were winging at the Lynch brothers very-very-available looks. Meanwhile, Henry was trying to credit the brothers' gloss on a union payoff he had witnessed that morning. Tearing himself away from speculating whether he could hit the Bronx by throwing a baseball across the Harlem River, Henry entered the dispatch shack just as Stancik, the district union rep, hefted a box-type briefcase and departed.

"And he ain't even packing," said the load manager. Which was how Henry surmised cash-in-the-bag.

"So the name of this chick is what?" said Frank. "The one you're going out with?" Molly, from the other office trailer, swore she had seen Henry's name in the *Daily News*.

Through the window of the Bull and Bear, Ray Levin watched Henry Birdsall cross Lexington Avenue. To the barman Ray signaled for the check. The cocktail waitress approached in step with Henry.

"Comped?" Henry nodded. Ray looked up at the waitress. "Thank you." Henry sat down. "Actually," said Ray, "we might not be done yet. How does it work?" he said to Henry.

"Just let me know," said the waitress, moving away.

"I got lucky. Guy signs in, desk clerk says, 'Have a nice stay, Mr. Stancik. Compliments of Mr. Fitzgerald.'"

"He said that?"

"Stancik goes, 'Thanks, buddy.' Then, 'Meals?' Gets a nod from the clerk, who by this time sees me standing there. A hundred and ninety bucks a night. Plus whatever he puts into his face in the dining room."

"This goes to a judge."

"Could I have," Henry called to the waitress, "like, a ginger ale?" He turned back to Ray. "Dicko's dialed it down to a dull roar with the no-shows. The union payoffs, I am at large on. But not this. This, Ray, I saw."

Outside, Henry pulled Ray to the curb. "I'm sick being bullshitted by these Irish. Dicko'll have some preposterous explanation for comping Stancik. I've been here before. I'm tired of not seeing what I saw."

"What do you mean, 'been here before?' In another life? Look, let me clear something up for you. Union leaders are prohibited from accepting cash gifts in any value whatsoever from wage-payers to membership. Prohibited by law."

Back at Cross & Case, Ray sat in a Hepplewhite chair retained by Freddy from Arthur Tannenbaum's decorating scheme. "His ass is in a sling. What about yours?" Freddy said.

"Who?"

"Ray, who the fuck have I been talking about? Santa Claus?" He turned to Henry. "I bet they all look like my wife."

"Trust me, they don't, and I've never seen your wife."

"Drew Case," Freddy said to Ray. Then to Henry, "How do you know they don't if you've never seen her."

"What happened to 'I'm a leg man?'" Henry said. "Freddy, if you bit any of these women on the breast, they'd smack you into next week."

"So?" Freddy asked Ray.

"What? Oh, that," Ray said. "Lopate's lying under oath. We never took stock payments for services."

"What are you gonna say tomorrow in court?"

He sighed. "Were you listening, Ray?" Henry asked.

"About the Dicko strategy? Tell you the truth, no."

That evening Dora returned to the dining room once the plates had been cleared away. In a faraway mood Ray had cocked his chair to a view of lawn and trees. Dora lay her hand on the back of his neck. Into the deep of the summer foliage together they stared at fireflies brightly calling darkness out of the color green. "The good thing is," she said, "after tomorrow, it'll all be over and you can enjoy the rest of summer. Do you want me to stop? It's tense, your neck."

"You'll never believe this. That kid going out with the socialite? He stumbled on another malfeasance. We're taking it to the judge."

"But, Ray."

"No, no, not *that* judge. Different judge and it goes to him in writing. In the concrete business they don't tie you up with lawsuits. They tie you up, throw you in the river. This judge rules non-compliance, that's it for the appeal. These guys are going to be very, very unhappy."

"Ray, don't tell me this."

"I'm not involved. Really."

Suddenly perspective descended on Ray re his appearance tomorrow for the defense in the trial of Donald Lopate, Arturo Machado, Congressman Richard Lukens, Congressman Nestor Arroyo versus the State of New York. Although Ray was only tangentially involved in the matter of *Fitzgerald Sand & Stone v. The City of New York*, he could suffer consequences. Physical ones. Embarrassing to admit this, but the thought gave him a thrill. "Honey," said Dora.

"I know. And I love you, too."

"It's true," she said. "I do."

In what Ray believed to be a miracle of irony, all the hands on all the wrought-iron clocks on the Eleventh Floor of the New York State Courthouse had been twisted away from their faces, thereby rendering as timeless legal decisions handed down to anyone who had forgotten to strap on a watch. "Yeah, and if they do work," said his lawyer, "they tell the wrong time."

At the defense table the four bad boys hulked on their chairs like prize fighters. The judge motioned prosecution and defense counsel to the bench. Ray took the stand and was sworn in. Viewed from the witness box, the judge, a woman, seemed almost attractive, a young school teacher. Finally, however, Ray knew fear.

Into the trial transcript went established facts of the case: the "comfort letter" to investors pursuant to the Armor Tech bond issue; the subsequent under-subscription of the offering; the withdrawal by the Small Business Administration of the Minority Business designation for Armor Tech. Ray's testimony had been designed to refute the contention that payments in shares of Armor Tech stock had been made to Cross & Case for services rendered.

"Did you, at any time, falsify data which would have materially affected the capability of Armor Technical to attract outside investment?" asked the defense lawyer.

Ray answered in the expected manner.

"What would have been the personal advantage to you, as an executive of Cross & Case, to have encouraged investment in the Armor Technical underwriting?"

"None," said Ray.

"And did you?" asked the judge. "Hurt your reputation by signing off on a document that allowed this particular company to be 'put into play.'"

"In my estimation, yes," said Ray.

Taking a sip of water, he now waited for the prosecution to swing its axe. "Were you aware, Mr. Levin," said the prosecutor, "that Drew Case, a name partner of your firm, owned shares of stock in Armor Technical?"

Ray found it surprisingly easy to lie. "No, I was not."

"You never discussed with Mr. Case his ownership of shares of Armor Tech stock?"

"I think I would have remembered."

"Never once did you discuss this with him?"

"No, I did not."

The prosecutor moved on to other questions and finally rested his cross. Left uncoupled was the connection between Drew's Armor Tech stock shares and the comfort letter, thereby preserving the ice under the skates of all concerned at Cross & Case.

But having vanished over the horizon of moral relativity, Ray now understood the concept of curvature of the earth. Half-jigging down the courthouse steps in the company of his lawyer, he could barely wait to catch the train home; kiss his two daughters and embrace his wife. Taking the long way around, he had returned to their world.

"**D**idn't you used to work there, Birdsy?"

"What are you talking about? You mean in the papers? You mean Armor Tech?"

"You gonna be famous?" asked Al.

"No. And I'm not going to jail either."

Al laughed. "So where you working now?"

Birdsall groaned. "You don't want to know."

They were driving to Chappaqua for a doubleheader, the clouds predictive of rain. Games, no games: Al did not care either way, a development that saddened him. The competition surpassed what he remembered, but rooted in a won-lost record of five and twelve was his conviction that his new Browns would never beat these teams that had played together for years. He would have felt even more bereft had it not become obvious to the entire Colonial League that he could still hit.

"You bring the sheet?" Birdsall asked.

"You're not gonna want to see it."

"Yeah, I know," said Henry, staring out the window. The sheet listed team batting and pitching stats, the rich/poor gap between everyone else and Al.

"Pretty quiet in here," said Al ten minutes later. "We ain't headed for Sing Sing. Although maybe Birdsall is."

"Say, what?" said Davy Rivera.

"Birdsy, reach in my bag, pass 'em out. You're in right today. I'm letting Boog play first."

"Fuck," said Sonny Suarez. "We might as well go home."

"So try not bouncing your throws."

A Browns uniform had bewitched Bill Baker out of his Baltimore Orioles costume, although he continued to wear the warm-up jacket, which was then often hidden by his teammates when he was up at the plate. Returning to the bench after "Strike Three" or a pop-up no higher than a child could throw,

Bill would ask, "Yo, anybody seen my, you know. My thing?"

"What thing, Boog?"

"Come on, man."

So heart-rending was Boog's anxiety that usually Birdsall would spill the beans. "Behind Al's cart, Boog, in Eddie's bag."

Eddie, throwing his last warm-up pitches, would glare over at Henry, taking infield at first. "Why'd you tell him?"

"You want him thinking about his jacket he gets a fly ball?"

Al would feel the gorge of indignation rising in his chest. The loss of Elizabeth had become mixed up with this travesty of Browns baseball, with Boog, the final insult. Loathe to descend into pickup-softball-game unseriousness by identifying Boog on the line-up card as "Boog," Al struggled to remember his name, having once had to go so far as to ask him to spell it.

"Bill," said Boog, confused, "Baker, B-a-k-e-r."

"Al thought it was maybe the French way, Boog."

On game days, Al had taken to leaving his dogs in the apartment. When he came home in the early evening, they were often asleep. Exhausted, depressed, he would sometimes fall to his knees to hug them both, trying to hold tightly to a moment as he, himself, slipped out of his grasp.

The Chappaqua team today featured a catcher from the Detroit Tigers system, down just this week from Triple-A, a big bronze god of an athlete embarking on the rest of his life. After he nailed two Browns trying to steal and, throwing from his knees, picked one off at second base, Lonnie Dixon inquired, "How many like him are in this league?"

Earlier, after pre-game warm-ups, Al's players, slumped on the dugout bench, all stared the same direction. Trim, muscular, and fond of very short gym trunks, Marty Kent could throw hard enough and throw strikes. His profession had been posited as male stripper by the other Browns. One look at the blonde with him now rested the prosecution's case.

"Pay attention," said Al, "we got a game to play."

But his own gaze, to the amusement of his players, had not yet abandoned the blonde. Extremely tall, she was dressed perfectly for three hundred degree weather in tiny scraps of clothing that went well with her infinitesimally thin ankle chain.

"She dances at this club I manage in Queens," said Marty, scheduled to pitch the back end of the doubleheader. "Name's Irina. Al, you think maybe I could pinch-hit the first game? Play a little outfield?"

Al pointed out that unless Marty got knocked out of the box in the second game, Irina would have plenty of opportunity to watch him perform.

"She might not stay that long."

"Go sit in the stands, Marty."

Thunder rumbled continuously through both games. Sweat boiled down Al's arms at second base and heat stroke seemed a real possibility, especially for the outfielders after Eddie Perez blew up in the fourth inning and had to be relieved.

"I need to sit down," said Eddie, tossing Al the ball and lurching gratefully off the mound. Lonnie Dixon finished up on the hill and hit a very long triple. The final score, 13-4.

"How is this prepared?" asked Marty.

"What?"

"The fried chicken."

Birdsall had brought a bagful of breasts cooked by his girlfriend. Or rather, as it developed under increasingly awed questioning, cooked by the kitchen staff of the grandparents of his girlfriend.

"What do you mean, 'prepared?' How is it cooked?"

"I don't eat fried foods unless they're prepared in low sodium, low fat olive oil." Marty followed the gaze of several players to the blonde girl, unfolding herself like a deck chair over several bleacher rows. "Irina doesn't either."

"Yes, I can see that," said Al.

The second game went slightly better than the first, the Triple-A catcher still putting on a clinic, but the Browns not decomposing quite so quickly. The experiment with Boog at first base had resulted in several sure put-outs caroming off his giant mitt. But then to the shock of his teammates, he turned a double-play. A "Boog" chant went up weakly from the spares in the dugout, not at all unhappy not to be on the field.

Then, in the next inning, Al looked up to see Boog jogging wide into the first base turn. The unexpectedness of the familiar kept him from realizing what had just occurred. But now he noticed the left fielder facing the outfield fence.

"Holy shit!" said Davey Rivera.

Jogging around second base with a little stutter step he had no doubt seen on TV, Bill Baker, "Boog," had hit a homerun. Rounding third, lost in a thousand boyhood dreams, he headed for the plate. Drained, defeated, about to be defeated again, the Browns crowded out of the dugout to greet him, laughing and stunned.

"It was like seeing a unicorn," said Birdsall, as they drove back to the city.

"Afterwards I seen him out there trying to find the ball," said Lonnie.

"Not gonna be here next weekend, Al" said Spider Givens. "Got family coming in."

"Okay." But Al was remembering Boog's look of primitive wonder as he landed his long cleated feet on the inverted white house of "home."

"Did he find it?" asked Birdsall

"The ball? Yeah, I think he did," Lonnie said.

"**C**ome here," said Dicko, pushing Henry along the office corridor.

At the elevator bank Henry said, "We're going somewhere, right, Dicko?"

In the elevator Henry said, "This is not the same judge as the one hearing your appeal. Although if he's upset enough, he'll probably rule in contempt."

"Out," said Dicko. A meaty hand forking his elbow, Henry departed the elevator. Then the building. "Over there," said Dicko, pointing. A black Lincoln stood at the curb.

"The New England," Dicko said to the driver. "Exit 33. After that I'll give you where."

"Look, Dicko, the non-compliance thing? I had to."

"Fuck you, you had to, but we won't get into that now."

Half an hour later, Dicko leaned forward to the driver. "Bottom of the ramp, turn left." The glide of the world decelerated. "Welcome to Rye," said a sign by the side of the road. "Second light," said Dicko, "hang a right."

When they entered the foyer of his Georgian mansion, Dicko announced to the house he was home. A cocker spaniel clicked across a herringbone wood floor, but Dicko was too busy flipping through his mail to pet him, so Henry did. On the patio, a glass of ice tea in hand, Sharon Fitzgerald glanced up at the unexpected appearance of her husband. "Where're the kids? Hello, Dorothy," said Dicko to the woman with Sharon.

Dicko's wife wore white chinos and a sleeveless blouse. Her beautiful feet in sandals completed the *tableaux*: Suburban Nymph at Rest. Working in concert with the many blondes of her hair was the freckled paleness of her skin.

Dicko threw himself into a chair, held up an envelope. "Why's this coming to the house?"

"So you can take care of it," she said wearily.

Her friend, exactly half as pretty as Sharon, smiled.

"Brendan went into town to buy... something," Sharon said. "Otis drove him. And Caroline has swimming practice, remember?"

"Yeah, sure," said Dicko.

"No, you don't." She looked at her watch. "I should pick her up, actually." Her friend, Dorothy, gulping the last of her wine cooler, dispensed altogether with the watch-checking fiction. "I've got to run, too," she said.

"Unless *you* want to pick her up."

Regretfully, Dicko interrupted his re-examination of the mail. "Can't," he said. Lawsuits and bankruptcy seemed less vexing to him than the emotional requirements of marriage.

When the women departed, he stood up. "Let's go."

Down a long stretch of grass Henry followed him towards a pond at the bottom of the property.

"You could play football on this lawn," Henry observed.

"The New York Giant cheerleaders? She hired 'em once, pompoms and all, to give me a 'Happy Birthday, Dicko' cheer. Right here. Right where you're standing. So it's not all rocky road for her. Apart from right now."

"You can't keep doing this, Dicko."

"Do you know any fucking thing at all?"

"I know what I saw."

Dicko yanked out his wallet. "Father and Daughter Dance. Look at her! She's beautiful, right? Takes after her mother. I had to resign the Mercy College Board. The Country Club? I'm on the Finance Committee. Now that's gone. My brothers and I, we tore our pants horsing around, we had to walk to school, save the carfare, buy another pair. Don't tell me about keeping my nose clean. You don't know clean. Not in concrete, you don't."

"Union payoffs? No-shows?"

"We're bending it, not breaking it."

"So let the judge made the call."

Dicko stared at him. "How's your parking garage?"

"My thing I'm working on?" Henry paused. "Fine."

Dicko smirked. "Yeah, sure. This is not a threat, okay? So don't go running to the judge. There's consequences to what you did. And not just to me."

As Henry returned to the black car parked in the driveway, the smell of Dicko's house brought back to him his visit to Rebecca's grandparents' summer castle on the Hudson. Dinner that first night was served in a dining room championed by stained glass doors. "Are those Tiffany?" Henry asked.

Rebecca giggled. "Henry's feeling socially insecure."

"Louis Tiffany or his workshop," said Priscilla Van Rijn graciously. "We were never quite sure."

"Yes, we were," said Rebecca.

"Do you hunt," rumbled Rebecca's grandfather, "Henry? After all, you grew up in the West."

"Do you hunt *Henry?*"

"Rebecca!" said her grandmother.

"Birds, yes, but not for a long time. Why?"

"What about fishing?"

"Grandfather wants to know if you'll row him around."

"Did you play sports, Mr. Van Rijn. At Harvard."

"Seventh oar," said Priscilla proudly. "And football."

"In those days," said Livingston Van Rijn, "we had a team for those of us weighing 150 pounds or less. Yale and your school had them, too. A kind of under-varsity."

"How nice," said Henry brainlessly.

Later, he suffered a lecture from Rebecca on the subject of not acting so nervous in front of her grandparents.

"How about cowed?" he suggested.

"Almost."

"Can I just say one thing? Your help meant everything."

"You're really cute when you're not quite sure of yourself."

"What's the room-sneaking-into situation around here?"

"Excellent," she said.

"Remind me not to ask you how you know."

Later still, he surprised Mrs. Van Rijn in the kitchen. In a fluffy white terrycloth robe, her bone structure revealed by the burnish of a skin-care unguent, she displayed no discomfiture at his unexpected presence. "Please help yourself, Henry. Lavinia has left us two crème brulee's."

"Thank you, I will."

"Rebecca seems quite fond of you."

"As I am of her." The actual sentiments, though, beneath the spoken ones, went something like this: *She's young, take care not to hurt her/I won't, I promise.*

"Goodnight, Henry. Sleep well."

Returning to his room, he made his way after safe interval to the bedroom where Rebecca awaited. "What took you so long," she said.

While being driven back to Manhattan in Dicko's black Lincoln, Henry realized why the same smell existed in the two houses. In both Rhinebeck and Rye he had passed through lingering veils of his own fear. For some reason he was unafraid of whatever Dicko might do to him, or even Priscilla Van Rijn. But his self-confidence, he suspected, was grievously misplaced and his fearlessness terrified him.

C andy, luxuriating on the couch, paddled her feet. "Can't we have them come over here? Have dinner at Café Central and then I'll head home?"

"You don't have to keep saying that, 'I'll head home.'"

Sarah left the room to use the phone in the foyer.

"But that's okay," Candy called to her, "wherever you want to go." Sarah heard her stretch, then the unmistakeable cheep of a fart. "Oh, goodness," said Candy.

"There was something you wanted to ask me?" said Sarah to Henry in an Upper East Side restaurant, the glow on Candy's face having intensified from realizing her dinner partner was Rebecca Van Rijn.

"I told you, didn't I, about the non-compliance memo? I did, right? Anyway," he said, "I had a little 'accident.'"

"By the way, how's your jackhammering buddy?"

"Who?" said Rebecca.

"Remember cash-in-a-briefcase? You saw in the papers, right, where Armor Tech was bribing guys at the Pentagon?"

"I did, yes. Ray told you he testified," said Sarah.

"Which is why I'm talking to you. He's busy enough."

"I'll have the *insalata caprese*," said Candy, "to start."

The waiter departed. Henry leaned forward, charmed to be the center of interest for three women. He turned to Rebecca. "You ordered?"

"Come on, Henry, quit it."

He sighed. "Okay, I'm walking to where my car's parked. After work, this is, in the Bronx." To Candy, he explained, "I'm monitoring a compliance order on a concrete company. They're appealing a judgment." Rebecca caught Sarah's eye, shook her head. "I saw that," said Henry. "Listen, everybody needs to be on the same page."

"Then turn it, for God's sake!"

"I'm making this sound like a joke, but it wasn't funny. I'm parked by one of the sand dumps. Next thing I know I'm flying through the air."

"No you weren't," said Rebecca.

"Bang! I bounce off my car. Two feet away is the crane clamshell. Straight down from the boom the fucking thing had dropped. I must have heard the chain rattle just before. These things are huge, the clams. But here's what's strange. Thank you," he said to the waiter. The appetizer, the second round of drinks had been set down. Candy tucked into her *caprese*, her eyes on Birdsall's face. "The guy in the crane cab? This is the strange thing. Normally, in this environment. They're all Irish up there," he said to Candy. "Normally, he would have been laughing. Near death industrial accident? This qualifies as humor to these assholes. But he's just staring at me. Right through the window of the cab. Staring at me."

"Any witnesses?" said Sarah

Birdsall shook his head. "There's a mechanism where they can drop the clam for cleaning it."

"You say anything to the crane operator?" Sarah asked.

"Absolutely. I picked myself up, got in my car. All the way home, I called him a motherfucking cocksucker."

"When did this happen?" asked Rebecca.

"Couple days ago. Next morning I told two of the guys I have a drink with sometimes, 'The armature's loose on one of the clams.' 'So we heard,' they said. That was it, 'So we heard.'"

"You've been keeping secrets," Rebecca said nervously.

"My advice?" said Sarah. "Don't walk next to any large machinery. And whatever you do, don't stay late."

"You ever get threats?" Henry asked.

The two young women stared at her. Sarah nodded. "Write down times and dates, describe what happened. Make copies. Accessible copies."

"And tell your boss," said Rebecca. "The one I met.

"That count being appealed," said Sarah. "Are they?"

"Price fixing? You know what? I'd like to find out."

As they left the restaurant she pulled Henry aside. "You're

a shit-magnet, aren't you?"

"Meaning what?"

"A tendency to draw events. I've seen it with cops."

In the cab Candy said, "I liked her. Very natural. But, of course, you lead such an interesting life." The throb in Candy's voice fidded notably with Sarah's organs below the heart.

Later, lying in bed, sheet between her legs, Sarah knew she could have Candy whenever she wanted. Out of context, the words delighted her: candy whenever she wanted. Finding her nipple through her nightgown's fabric, she was more than ready for the softness of female sex.

Standing by the Museum subway entrance, she had asked Candy, "Did I tell you about my co-op interview?"

"No, you didn't."

"I was nervous about what I should wear. So I thought, 'why not dress up the lawyer thing a bit?' Leather, I was thinking. A very thin black leather raincoat I saw in Bendel's. These interviews are not quite a pap test, but you get the idea. One of the board members, I quite charmed him, although I'm sure he's gay, he helps me on afterwards with my raincoat. We all say goodbye, and then back at my apartment..."

"The one you're in now."

"... when I'm putting the raincoat away, I notice the price tag hanging out the back. I was so embarrassed. That'll teach me, I thought. Trying to be something I'm not.'"

"But you passed."

"Naturally. Goodnight, dear." As she leaned in to kiss Candy on the cheek, Candy moved her head slightly so that Sarah's kiss landed half on her mouth.

Rebecca had not given life after college much thought. Two girls she knew from Dalton and the brother of a Harvard classmate wanted to share an apartment with her. She had agreed to veto or approve choices, but held her options open for now, unsure what her future with Henry held.

"You're too young," said her Aunt Clara. "Believe me, he'll wait until you're ready, and if he won't, you'll find someone else. Which reminds me, what does he want to do in life?"

"He has an MBA."

"Rebecca, please. Can't you be more specific? I hope he can. Although I do think older is a good idea for you."

They were having tea in her grandparents' living room, Harriet bustling around in the early stages of cocktail party preparation. "He is coming tonight, your friend?" she asked Rebecca. "*Non*," she said to the maid, moving the flowers to a sideboard. "This, they will knock over."

"Harriet, how do you say, '*Henri*,' in your language?"

Harriet did an annoyed-French-person face. She liked Henry, but would never presume to advise Rebecca about men

"I *wish* they'd drop a clamshell on my head," said Henry that afternoon. "That way I wouldn't have to go home."

"Really?"

"My sister, my brother. Every so often it's contractually required. What's the matter with you?"

"Nothing."

"Bullshit."

"You should have asked me to go."

"Perhaps you're confusing Pennsylvania with Paris."

"Okay, don't take me then."

But both knew they had reached a relationship crossroads. He cocked his head. "Actually, I'd love it if you came."

His father, Buster, tall and rosy, was an absentminded professor type. His mother was small, dark and dangerous.

"I'm so happy Henry would bring you along," said Guinivere-please-call-me-Gwen, depositing Rebecca in a guest room, miles away from her son.

"What about the downstairs one," Henry said.

"This is nice," said Rebecca, signaling cease-and-desist.

"I don't see why not," Henry persisted.

"Because," said his mother. "Not."

"Fine. I'll sneak up the stairs."

"No, you won't," said his mother, with a glint in her eye.

Rebecca was speechless with embarrassment.

In the living room, Henry's sister Bobbie stepped back to regard Rebecca with the self-conscious intensity of a portrait photographer. Instantly, Rebecca liked her.

"Bobbie's an alcoholic," said Henry.

"And don't forget married three times."

"Speaking of which."

"No, this one I buried in the garden. Henry, for Christ's sake, make her a drink, before she really needs one."

"Who's this Theodore person?"

"He didn't tell you? He wants to show you off to the entire family."

The arrival of Theodore, the older brother, and his wife plunged dinner into a mid-air stall. As a matter of nostalgia, Rebecca had been quizzing Buster about his invention of the Slinky. "Except he didn't renew the patent," said Henry

"You'd be surprised to hear how much I sold it for."

"Let's not be surprised," said Gwen quickly

"We met at Harvard," Ted's wife, Elaine, told Rebecca, with a nod towards her spouse, who kept referring to himself, ponderously, as "Ted, the oldest child." Discourse at the dinner table had degenerated by then into the sort of recaps which summarize previous television episodes.

Gradually, the weekend improved. Elaine discussed with Rebecca medieval epistemology, her Senior Thesis. Her two little boys seemed simply that. Little boys. Ted, behind his ho-

ho-ho stolidity, retained an unalarmed affection for his younger brother. Guinivere made her cry once, which no one saw, because Rebecca fled the house while Henry scolded his mother, who nevertheless continued to emotionally exclude her and was thus folded away into the same psychological foot locker where Rebecca kept her mother. Buster had known friends of her father's at Harvard and thus did he easily step into the outline of her father.

Fragile from carousing with Henry and Bobbie, Rebecca floated in the pool on an inflatable raft. Henry had cleared her head of cobwebs an hour earlier with a short intense session on the edge of a four-poster bed. Watching him now, sunning on a chaise, she suffered a stab of regret. The comforting tumult of cousins and aunts would be impossible here. A tragedy-less family like Henry's could never be a complement to her own. Isolated from each other and therefore immune to loss, they led an oddly deprived existence.

The afternoon Rebecca and Henry departed, Guinivere gave her a hug. "Come back," she said, waving goodbye with a tissue scrap, which indicated to Rebecca, tears. This was the kind of stunt her mother would have pulled. The smack, then the kiss. The sight of Henry's little nephews reminded Rebecca of her own childhood, before her parents died. She had been blank-faced and trusting, too.

"I'm serious," Buster said to Henry. "The path of least resistance is the path these people take. Don't be foolish."

"Did you say goodbye to Rebecca?"

"Foolish about what?" she asked as they drove away.

"Talking to other concrete guys about this price-fixing thing." Henry was annoyed at his father and Rebecca knew why. The minute she came into anyone's life, the people who loved that person immediately loved them more.

In the thunderous heat of full summer Henry's work in the Bronx surrendered to routine. Once Dicko and his lawyers subsided into aggrieved damage control, the atmosphere in the trailers improved.

"It's your job," said Pete McCann, "blowing the whistle."

"Thank you," said Henry.

Pete climbed into the cab of his transit mixer, the innards of his drum jackhammered clear. Convinced that the man was undercover NYPD, Henry was told the real story by Molly Lynch, Frank's wife, who had now seen Henry's name twice in the *Post* in association with Rebecca Van Rijn.

"What's she like? All of us want to know."

"Nice."

"So I guess we'll be using the blowtorch then. We'll need more than that, Henry."

"Okay. Very nice."

The air-conditioning was less aggressive in Molly's trailer so Henry found reasons to visit. "The true Pete story?" she said. "The one we hear is true, anyway."

"Is he an undercover cop?"

"You'd like that, wouldn't you? Makes you not the only fink on the lot. No, but he *was* undercover. Robbery detail last Christmas. In the papers, this was. But not the really awful part. That mall out there used to be Roosevelt Field? Pete's in the red suit, the fluffy white beard. They pull a job, the crooks, they're getting away and Pete's shot hits a little boy. This is the part not in the papers. 'Why'd you shoot me, Santa,' the little boy says. Can you imagine? 'Why'd you shoot me, Santa?'"

"Who told you this?" Given his experience with these Irish untrustworthies, Henry suspected leg-pulling.

"My aunt. Which reminds me."

"Not Frank or Jackie?"

She grimaced. "Well, you can't very well ask Pete now, can you? Which reminds me, though. Your girlfriend? You go out every night?"

"No fix-ups, okay? I'm not interested."

"*Not* a fix-up is what I'm saying. Frank's cousin, Nina Murray, terrifically pretty girl. She makes these documentaries they're called. I gather she's quite the thing in her business."

"'Nina Murray.' Name's pretty, anyway. But, no."

"Would you listen! I'm not talking 'date,' for fuck's sake! Christine, tell him I'm not. Frank's cousin. She's invited to all sorts of fanciness, but doesn't want to go with some fool constantly hitting on her. She wants a man who's 'taken,' don't you see? Which fits the bill of you."

"Is this a bribe?"

"Oh, the hell with you. She's a lovely person."

"A bribe so you'll tell us more about Rebecca?" inquired Christine. "You're quite close-mouthed, you know. We're not good enough for you? Is that it, Henry?"

"That's it. Frank's cousin. Sure. Maybe."

"Don't do us any favors," said Molly.

Driving back from Southhampton with Rebecca, Henry blurted out, "What the hell do they want?"

"They think I'm too young."

"Your aunts?"

"And uncles. But not all of them."

"Don't tell me which ones because it'll just change."

She laughed. "Your family's not like that?"

"Do you really want to go to law school?"

Headlights washed over her face. "I want to be with you." Inside him, the wind shifted. He reached across the seat, took her hand. "I do," she said.

"I love you."

"I'm old enough. I know what I want. We'll tell them."

"Have you told your grandmother?"

"I was surprised. She thought it was okay. But she said we won't make any announcements just yet. She even thought maybe we should live together first."

"There's an idea," said Henry doubtfully.

After an engagement party for Rebecca's cousin, Laura, Henry complained, "They're dipsticking me for malleability. They want to know if I'm squeezable into a slot."

"Into one of the family companies, you mean?"

"It's what they're doing," he said. "I'm cannon fodder."

A week later, he drove out to Queens. A competitor of Dicko's, John Initaglia, had called to say a few nice words about "the big Irishman." When Henry brought up price-fixing, Initaglia passed on the phone number of another concrete king, Russ Cangelosi. The interview in Cangelosi's office on Jamaica Bay went poorly enough that Henry finally glanced out the window and wisecracked, "Who's the fat girl?"

Cangelosi sighed. "Typical fucking Irish."

"Which I'm not even."

"Makes it worse. The 'fat girl?' Nellie Santoro. Guy with him? Jimmy Tontino. Why? You wanna talk to 'em?"

"I notice they're in suits. We'll compare tailoring."

"You'll lose."

Out the window behind Cangelosi stood two Italians, one the size of a hotdog cart, the other skinny, both acting unobvious enough to be occupationally obvious. They had exchanged looks with Henry on his walk to Cangelosi's office, which was a barracks-like structure, a relic of the Second World War. Coming from two mafiosi, the looks seemed surprisingly mild. To them Henry was just another clown in a business suit, although, crucially, non-law enforcement.

"Look, I know it's a tough business," Henry said.

"So what are you coming to me for, you already know."

"That's a good question."

A better question, he reflected, was why he felt impervious to physical harm. His pell-mell foolhardiness had led Henry to suspect himself of harboring a deathwish. Perhaps he and Dicko in father-son contests wrestled on adjoining mats: Dicko, the inky shadow of his father's probity; Henry, the flesh of his father's shadow.

Cangelosi stood up. "I'll walk you out."

As they crossed the workyard, the two mobsters drove off in a new Cadillac.

"This piece of shit?" said Cangelosi when they reached Henry's Fiat. "You can't afford a better car?"

"Not really."

Cangelosi squinted into the distance. Henry sensed a draft of decency here. "Bids are sealed on the big jobs, low ball wins. Sure there's price-fixing. We all do it if we can. That City lawsuit? You're pissing up a rope. But you get paid for it, right? They ought to pay you enough, get another car."

Henry laughed. "You mind I keep in touch?"

"Suit yourself."

"So the question is," said Ray, "is Dicko dirty on the price fixing or anything else? And number two, why isn't the judge hitting him on cash-in-the-bag."

"You mean comped hotel rooms?"

"Or feeding your memo to the appeals judge? That stone's not still falling, believe me. It just never splashed."

"They all 'price-fix.' Whatever the fuck that means."

Ray consulted his desk calendar. "Ruling expected early September. That's the end of the tunnel for us."

"Speaking of tunnel. He's got another company, Water Tunnel. A blizzard of checks going back and forth between them and Sand & Stone."

They sat in Ray's new office, slightly bigger than his last one, evidence of a change in career weather now that the Armor Tech trial was winding down. Ray yawned. "Look, Dicko's clean on the no-shows. You blew the whistle on the union stuff. Sound of one hand clapping so far."

"One of Dicko's nephews? He's got a cousin. The guy's wife, this is, trying to set me up with her. They're running some kind of game."

"What happened to the famous one?"

"Moving forward is all I can say."

"Really?" said Ray.

"I still feel bad about Artie Machado. Lopate, I never liked. They're gonna nail these guys, aren't they?"

"It'll go worse for the two congressmen. You know what I think? I think I'll tag along."

"To Dicko's? Help yourself."

For moments at a time, clothes shopping with Dora or on the beach with his little girls, Ray had gone deaf to the ticking clock of Armor Tech and dumb to the consequences of his lie on the witness stand.

"What's up with your *lis*?" Birdsall asked Dicko.

"Fucker's judgment-proof. So why the visit? No, sit over here." Ray and Henry had taken seats on the couch next to Dicko's desk. Dutifully, they waggled their asses closer. Henry nodded at the desk. "You taping us, Dicko? I bet you are."

"To what do I owe the pleasure?" said Dicko grandly.

Ray handed him Henry's latest monthly report. "And a copy to Judge Bryant."

"Mind if I read the fucking thing."

"Did you test the audio level first? I bet you didn't."

After flipping through the report, Dicko glanced at Henry and Ray. "That's why you came up here?"

"Since when is all A's on your report card's a problem?"

"So this is what? Some sort of olive branch?"

"And Initaglia called me. Who's next, the parish priest?"

Dicko grinned. "I'm a beloved person."

"So why hide the microphone, you're so beloved?"

"Listen, asshole, you know I don't trust you."

"Without consent, taping does not hold up in court."

"Yes, it does. In transcript."

"Fine," said Birdsall, bending to the desk drawer. "I hereby grant my consent."

Ray took a deep breath. "Speaking of court, Henry says your competitors back you up on this price-fixing charge.

"Waiting in the hallway to testify and my fucking lawyer didn't put 'em on! Some bullshit about 'public perception.'" Dicko stood up. "Birdsall, this fancy-ass chick you're going out with, she know how crazy you are?"

"She should meet you, she wants crazy."

"Bring her around when I'm divorced. Yeah, talk to Sharon. Too much on my plate. No time for her, she says."

Dicko shepherded Ray and Henry to the door. Phones were ringing. Two men queued in the hall, one the comptroller, Merridew; the other, Hugh Lynch.

On the way to Reception Henry lowered his voice. "You saw the one looked like Cardinal O'Connor? Water Tunnel."

Henry indicated an office cubicle. On a file cabinet neatly packed into a copypaper box was a corduroy road of Water Tunnel check envelopes, addressed to branch after branch of Chemical Bank. Ray looked up from the envelopes at Henry.

"Runs all his businesses out of here?"

"Hotel, furniture factory, fish meal plant, restaurant chain in Florida, and this Water Tunnel. He's teaching me."

The elevator arrived, other passengers on the car.

"Teaching you what?" Ray asked outside.

"To be a businessman. Except in reverse."

Ray smiled. Out of grunt work emerged at last the dollars and cents personalities people like Henry would employ in the business world. Experience did this, yes, but definitely Ray felt the thrill of responsibility. "Dora's coming in. You want to join us? Say 6:30. At Dean's?"

"Why not. We haven't been for a while."

Certainly, Birdsall was no one to set your watch by, but Ray would enjoy seeing the shock and pleasure on Dora's face if Rebecca Van Rijn showed up.

Late that afternoon the verdicts came in. Although prison time for the defendants appeared unlikely, all were ruined by mixed count convictions. Lopate probably would serve time for perjury; the staffs of the two congressmen had already prepared resignation documents; Artie Machado announced his intention to appeal. Tomorrow's papers would undoubtedly savage Cross & Case for having the wool pulled over its eyes, but the meter was now running on Ray's reinstatement to full honors at the firm. Dora called. "Is it over?"

"This part is."

"What do you mean, 'this part?'"

"It's over. See you tonight."

Freddy Habyan and Mike Peruwitz came by to congratulate him. Ray quelled the urge to call Drew Case, and then was "in a meeting" to Drew's call.

With the girls away at summer camp, Ray and Dora had fallen into a greater intimacy and he now saw Dean's through her eyes. Suddenly the place seemed shabby and emotionally unnecessary and Irish to a sad fault. His secret about the Van Rijn girl held, but its effect at reveal did not rise to the expected response. Rebecca's sudden ordinariness struck Ray as drastic. Gradually her looks reasserted themselves, but by then she was just another pretty girl.

After the theater, on the cab ride back to the hotel where they were "honeymooning," Dora even volunteered, "I don't see what's so special about her. Although she did seem nice. Maybe we just weren't her type."

"That's possible," he said.

"We're *old*," said Dora, coquettishly.

"You're not."

"You're not, either, Raymond." She took his hand.

In the looks and figure she still possessed, Ray mourned the loss of nearly half his life. And then, magically, he was satisfied with that, with the rightness of his predicate existence. In his moment of contentment, though, he found room to pity his *protege*. What in the world did life have in store for that poor guy if Rebecca van Rijn became Rebecca Birdsall?

Henry's fact finding forays now concealed West Side dock expeditions with representatives of moribund shipping companies and commercial real estate agents. Walking the rotting sheds on the rotting piers, he would pitch lease and purchase prices and possible participation by property owners, although rarely did he meet one of these except for May Roehmer, a Tugboat Annie, who even in the summer heat wore a shawl-necked sweater, dribbled down the front with cigarette ash.

"Gimme that," said May to Henry, who handed her his projections. Resurrecting a pencil from her sweater, she jotted down her own figures. Jabbed the pencil butt at the real estate agent. "Listen up, Pancho, me and boyfriend here might do business, we can agree on a price." She eyed Henry. "Not afraid of a little risk, are you? Well, are you?" she pressed after Henry remained mute, enraptured by the word 'risk.'

"Fuck, no!" he said. "I mean, 'No, I'm not."

"'Fuck, no' is fine. Call me May, by the way. So how much money can you raise?"

"About," Henry lied, "a hundred K."

"Bank draft or cash?"

When Henry hesitated, she shrugged. "Come by my office, you get the check. Meanwhile, think up a name for this folly."

"Throw a tent over this circus, you mean?"

"In so many words, yeah," she said, walking away. "Come up with a good one. Naming ain't my strong suit."

Stifling an impulse to yell after her, "Pier Parking, Inc.," his working title, Henry plunged into fretfulness at the impossibility of raising a hundred grand. The property was located in the West 20's of industrial Chelsea, an area not synonymous with personal safety or financial gain.

"So, Henry," said Molly Lynch, back in the Bronx, "what's

your schedule Sunday night."

"This Sunday night?"

"Quit stalling. Yes, or no."

"How'd you sneak in? I didn't even see the door open."

"'No,' then," she said, leaving the trailer.

A minute later, Henry stood before Molly's desk. "I don't know. Call me. I get back from playing around six."

"I hope you don't think that's a 'yes.' Mary," said Molly, handing a stack of check envelopes to one of her minions. "Deposits. On your horse." Mary Devine raised her long nose from a *sotto voce* conversation over the telephone. Molly turned to Henry. "Maybe we will, maybe we won't. Call."

"Hey," said Henry, annoyed, "usually I'm not free."

"Then next time check with your girlfriend."

Several days earlier, Henry and Rebecca had returned from dinner to her grandparents' Park Avenue apartment. With the Van Rijn seniors still in Rhinebeck, Rebecca kicked off her sandals, unbuttoned her cotton blouse. On the library couch, she flopped on top of Henry. "Grandmother thinks I've turned into cottage cheese. That I have no initiative. That I can't make up my mind. What's wrong?"

"Just that you're a little heavy. Not really heavy, but... no one believes in air-conditioning?"

"Why?" she said, bouncing on his lap. "You're hot?" Straddling him, her solid middle plunging him deeply into the seat cushion, she moved to dismount. But he restrained her, smelling the sweat on her skin where her blouse was open.

Down the hallway to her room they drifted. Talking about the future, they undressed. He went at her in his usual manner, but perhaps inspired by her earlier straddle, by the damp white space between her breasts, he rolled over on his back and placed her hands on his chest. She stopped, stared at him inquisitively, then lowered her head as though listening to a melody. Her hair swung back and forth. Although he could feel no difference in the clutch of her, obviously a moment had occurred. "My God," she said softly and shuddered. "I think," she said. "Yes, I think I had one."

"You're kidding."

"That was it," she said in a drowsy voice.

Awed and proud, she rolled off him and padded into the bathroom. Re-emerging, she climbed in beside him and they slept. He woke, dressed, departed. Instead of walking home he took a cab. He had passed on to her a physical knowledge, which now belonged entirely to her.

That Sunday the Browns had a doubleheader in Stamford, Connecticut on a diamond with concrete bleachers, chalked foul lines and a true backstop. Standing on second, watching Al work the count, Henry imagined that he and his teammates were the ceremonial fabrications of a long-vanished cult. Then Al clipped a line-drive single and Henry was too busy racing for home to remember how Stonehenge had visited him on the baseball field.

"Well?"

"Tonight? Sure."

"Be outside around seven."

An hour later, Henry climbed into the back seat of Frank Lynch's Chevy Impala. "Jesus, Frank," said Molly, "can we put the scooter in the trunk, for Christ's sake!"

"Will you listen to her?" said Frank. "No, we can't."

"Forget it," Henry said. "There's plenty of room."

"Idiots, the both of you. I've got kids coming out of my ears. We're on a date." Quickly, she turned to Henry. "No, not a date. Four people having dinner."

"So, Henry, you've seen this girl?"

Molly sighed. "Frank, please shut up."

As Henry stared out the window, his favorite song, "Heart of Glass," played on the radio. Once the glower of lower Park had succeeded the shiny blasted emptiness of midtown, they crept a side street below 23rd. Tall old factory windows stared from emporia which had once sold hats and gloves. Henry glanced at a shadow under a streetlight.

"There she is," said Molly.

The shadow turned at the approaching car. Henry could see nothing of her, really. All he sensed was a slimness of figure, small shoulders and a straight back. What she looked like meant little to him. Struck by her structural rectitude, by her *psychic* posture, he was quivering like a tuning fork.

"A documentary filmmaker," he said in preposterous awe.

"Henry, for Christ's sake, I already told you that."

Much of what transpired that evening occurred to him as prior knowledge. Despite her daunting self-possession, the young woman seemed indisputably a girl. Her swollen-eyed look, almost Asiatic, her darkly reddish hair, her long legs: these were elements of some importance, perhaps great importance, but Henry could only marvel at his first glimpse of her. Under a streetlight. In silhouette.

"I don't know," she said, "when I'm going back."

"Very impressive."

"Nicaragua? You never know what could happen, but I've been other places where fighting's going on."

A light rain had begun to glisten on the pavement. Frank was already behind the wheel. Watching Henry and Nina, Molly stood at the open passenger door, torn between amusement and contempt.

"I enjoyed meeting you," said Henry.

"So did I," she said. They shook hands. "Good luck."

"You, too," he said. "You'll need it more than I will."

She smiled and walked towards the car. She had lowered her head slightly, perhaps for the rain, but then Henry thought, no, not the rain. Instead in her gait he sensed her submission to an early sorrow. A thoughtful kind of courage to which she was condemned.

Frank and Molly, heading for the Tunnel, dropped her off. Henry Birdsall, future husband of Rebecca Van Rijn, took the subway home.

"Why don't you ask Buster for it."

"Pointless. But he'd give it to you."

"True," Bobbie said. "Want me to beat it out of him?" They were in a new cafe down the hill from his apartment. "What about her family? Wouldn't they come in for that? It's folding money to them."

"Down, boy. Besides, that doesn't feel right. We're not married, Bobbie."

"But you're going to be."

Henry toyed with blurting out, I met a girl. Met a girl what, however. Unsure how to treat what had occurred a few nights earlier he kept his counsel. Bobbie had come up from Ardmore to scout merchandise for a dog store she was opening with a Main Line rich woman with grown kids and therefore nothing to do. "Does Gwenny feel like you're replacing her?"

"With who? Gwen?"

"Come on! You didn't tell me that. Bullshit, you did! Your partner's name is Gwen?"

Bobbie laughed. "It's sick, isn't it? Of course, Gwenny, or should I say, Guinivere, is trying to co-opt her. Making a big effort to be friends."

"Is there some sort of lesbian term for 'Lucky Pierre?'"

"It's all we have since Baby Jesus left the creche."

"Yeah, well, not so fast. We're not formally."

"What, engaged? So? She's not statutory. What happened, she doesn't want to now?"

"She's having trouble making up her mind. Her whole fucking family's pulling her one way, then the other."

"Listen. Give her room. It'll just take time."

Once again, beneath the calm sureties of Henry's future marriage to Rebecca an emptiness of anxiety howled.

"Know why I'm up here? To get a breast exam."

103

"They look big enough to me. Oh, I thought you said 'job.' Why?" he said, regretting his flippancy.

"I want a second opinion."

Although Henry's day was occupied with its usual nonsense at Fitzgerald, he was now overwhelmed by his need to hear the name "Nina" spoken aloud.

"So when are you getting married?" Molly asked.

"Who wants to know?"

"Not Nina. The whole point, you might recall."

"What's with these checks you're always writing?"

"None of your business. And I mean that sincerely. You're a lost soul, Henry."

"Why, because I'm 'engaged?'"

"Because you don't know what's good for you."

"Would I have seen any of her documentaries?"

"If you're up for that sort of thing. PBS. Do you know that channel?"

"Please. So why all the checks? I ask Angie and Mary for back order tickets. They can't. Too busy writing checks."

Business diligence served as Henry's cloak for fact-finding forays about Nina Murray. What he was really looking for were reasons to void her eligibility for him, reasons to prefer the obvious choice, Rebecca.

"So," said Frank, "some sparks going off."

By accident, Henry had run across Frank and Jackie, returning from lunch. They now stood in the shade of a transit mixer. Henry shrugged. "Pretty girl."

"She is that," said Jackie.

"Bit of a stiff, though."

"Like how?" Henry's heart sank.

"Above herself. Mysterious," Frank said.

"Cut and dried," said Jackie. "Not much for the pail and pitcher crowd."

"He's taken, anyway, Jack."

Henry found himself studying Nina's cousins in search of her genes. Frank's thick-haired handsomeness rang a bell, but her genetic signature was more elusive in Jackie. Then it came to him: the slightly Mongolian eyes. Seeing her physiognomy in that of these men, he shivered with repulsion. "She won't step out with you, if that's what you're thinking," said Frank.

"She liked you, did she?" Jackie said.

Trying not to reveal his uncertainty on this point, Henry asked Frank, "Your Dad's company, Water Tunnel? What's with all these checks going back and forth?"

"Family flim-flam, I'm sure. Keeps his own counsel, Hugh does. He's your girlfriend's uncle, you know, Nina. Dicko's her second cousin."

"How old is she?"

"Middle 30's, I'd say."

Gladly, Henry accepted this news, hoping the slight age disparity would be enough to derail his interest. He then discovered in the outer office of Bobbie's gynecologist that his sympathy for women had expanded. He thought of his sister having her breasts palpated, followed by the radium barbeque of the mammogram. Pay attention to this separate heroism, a voice told him. "I will," he responded. Responded audibly, unfortunately, which merited him several alarmed glances from women in the waiting room.

"Thank God!" he said as he and Bobbie flagged down a cab. "Fibroid but not cancerous."

"So he thinks. But your opinion counts, too, nurse."

"You're coming with me tonight."

"What about girlfriend?"

"Out in Southhampton. You're gonna meet this guy."

Apart from its whiff of the incestuous, the dumbness of Henry's hopes for connecting his actual sister with his fantasy father figure became apparent about two minutes into the encounter at the Adage Lounge. A bronze girl appeared Henry mistook for Elizabeth until she was introduced. Carmen, who on second glance, was neither Latin nor out of her twenties.

"So I'm playing Fall League with the Robins," Al said.

"Sounds good. How's your political stuff, by the way?"

"I might be announcing. City Council."

"You got my vote. Unless that means I get jury duty."

"You're not in my district anyway."

"Here's what I'm looking for: 100K. Business deal. Know anybody?"

"My brother says you're gonna be mayor some day."

Carmen guffawed.

"Bobbie, shut up," said Henry.

"He tell you what a good hitter I am."

"Why, shut up? I'm sure he did."

"Birdsall, how long you been planning this?"

"What's he talking about?" said Carmen.

"I have an investor, but I'm on the hook for my share."

"What you think? I got that much lying around?"

"He does," said Carmen, "I need to hear about it."

"Use this investor secure you a loan. He covers your half. You make less, but you started. What's wrong with you?"

"See, Henry?" said his sister. "Problem solved."

Bobbie returned to Ardmore the next afternoon, and that night, strolling from the Adage Lounge, Al indicated to Henry, Carmen or no, he still carried a torch for Elizabeth.

"So did you miss me?" Rebecca said. "They all asked for you. Laura and Millie. Diana. Even Uncle George."

"I bet." Perhaps he was overconfident, but even in his dunderheadedness, he knew what he was doing. "I met a nice girl last weekend."

"Did you?"

Having grown up around philanderers, Rebecca thought she understood Henry's insecurity. To family females unfaithfulness was considered a mystery of gender, the male drive to dominate. Not that the scorned parties treated affairs lightly. Occasionally marriages broke up. Less frequent was slip-sliding about by Van Rijn women programmed to consider sexual acts as having similar health benefits to participation in sports.

"So how did you two meet?" Rebecca asked.

"You'd like her. She makes documentaries. She just came back from that war in Nicaragua."

"When does she return?" she asked the next afternoon.

"Who? To Nicaragua, you mean."

"Right away you knew who I was talking about."

"A cousin of theirs, okay? The people from the concrete plant. I'm still not sure what the motive was, except she's not mixed up in it." He sighed. "I know. The more I talk, the worse it sounds, right?"

Rebecca had recently discovered that Henry's continental shelf of beguiling attributes dropped off suddenly into murky cold darkness. Another Henry, ocean-going not pelagic, swam beneath his coral brightness.

"What the hell..." he said as they strolled on Fifth Avenue.

The lyric for "Heart of Glass" unrolled as she sang. To its rhythm she bumped him with her butt, which he tried to finesse with a wry smile. An uneasiness, though, peeked through his efforts at nonchalance.

Moments later he noted, "You can actually carry a tune."

That stopped her. A compliment from a man consumed with thoughts of another girl. "I've been invited to Morocco. Tangiers," she said. "I think I might go."

"Since when?"

"Sally Maxwell and her husband. They have a house."

"Good for them. But why?"

"So you can go on 'dates.'"

"I thought we were getting married."

"We are. After you've had a few more 'dates.'"

"I've had plenty, and can we drop the quotation marks?"

"They asked me last weekend. I've been thinking it over." He was making this easy for her, which angered her further. "Friends over there I haven't seen for a while."

Old boyfriend, he read correctly, but let the provocation pass. "For how long?"

"A couple weeks."

"Okay," he said. "Except I don't want you to go."

"I won't, then."

"Look, she's a career woman. Not the same background. You're what I want. And we have something. Go if you want to. If you feel you have to."

She surprised herself. "I think I should."

"But not because."

"No. Because afterward there won't be time for trips."

Later, her grandmother asked her, "How are things going with Henry, dear?"

"Fine." Then she added, "He understands me."

But walking with Henry now Rebecca imagined Mark sweating his white shirt transparent as he swung crates of medicine out of a jeep. Contrapuntally, her devotion to Henry increased. "You should have asked Uncle George for the money. You could have, you know. So when can I meet her?"

Henry, thinking she meant his friend, hesitated briefly, then recovered when Rebecca frowned. "May, you mean? As soon as you come back. Nobody else has. You'll be the first."

Before she left for Tangiers, Rebecca and Henry had lunch with Sarah, the lawyer, and her assistant. Convection winds bedeviled a hot Saturday afternoon. The paper table coverings flapped up at the edges, grit particles gathering like pencil lines, then dispersing when the creases blew flat.

"Something's up," Sarah said, finishing her *salade nicoise.*

"With the memo?"

"Absent a ruling, yes." Sarah turned to Rebecca. "The appeal should have been denied, the company put into receivership. Have you talked to Ray?" she said to Henry.

"You didn't call him?"

"Then pass this on. Federal racketeering probe. Or so I hear. Not exactly man-bites-dog in the construction trade. And not exactly a stretch to think your boy might be involved."

"What happens next?" Rebecca asked Henry later. "Are you in danger?" She was ready to cancel her trip and the next moment afraid he would ask her to.

"I doubt it."

The following night she was to leave for Tangiers. Apart from travel excitement, she felt a thrilling sense of fatedness with Henry. This I-met-a-nice-girl business presented only a twist in the narrative thread stretching out before them. Her grandparents had returned from Rhinebeck to wish her *bon voyage* so she and Henry trysted in his apartment.

He sat naked on his radiator cover. Suspecting his sudden remoteness, she wondered was he weighing potential damage from that federal business to the family of his friend. So what! Let him have his life, as she was about to have hers.

"I need to give you room," he said. "Time. To catch up." She was miffed. This had been *her* idea.

"I'm going to miss you," she said.

"I am, too… No, no. Come on. Don't."

"I can't help it." She wiped away tears. "I'm scared." He sat down beside her on the bed and held her. She stopped crying, began to laugh. "Silly," she said.

"Not really. But, yeah." Protected, she felt protective.

"You'll be okay, too," she said.

By posting nine wins against twenty-three losses, the New York Browns gained unchallenged possession of last place in the Colonial League. Al drove in his Bonneville down country roads to villages barely visible in the green cladding of summer. His city-boy Browns grew nervously reminiscent of sleep-over stories featuring axe *aficionados* in rural settings. Far back on tended lawns, white houses stood ramrod straight like dispersed Revolutionary soldiers awaiting command to ambush from the trees.

To take his mind off the despair of playing on a bad team, to quiet the gnaw of uncertainty over his higher office plans, Al would project himself into these clapboard lives. Surprisingly, the speculation proved restful, a compensation for the indignities suffered by his baseball dreams.

"Birdsy's gonna have to ask."

"Yeah, except we ain't lost."

"How you know we ain't? Black man asking directions up here? Be like a horror film."

"We're not lost, okay? And if we are, one of you racists can stand guard while the rest of us sleeps in the car."

Returning late to his apartment, Al would be greeted by sticky urine residues or crusted pyramids of shit. Upon him would descend the airlessness of his existence, his life reduced to his dogs and his health food store. A phone call to Elizabeth delivered his energies to more profitable ends. Briskly now he secured a dogsitter for Al and Benji so he could fly to L.A. for a few days.

"I don't want you staying here," she said on the phone.

"Did I say that? Did I?"

She laughed. "Then how come?"

"Curious about you people out there."

She laughed. "'You people.' Find you a hotel, though, that

I can do. Even see I can't dig you up a car. You might have to rent. You don't wanna be waiting on no bus."

"Hell. I had time, I'd drive out."

"What you up to, Al?" Her suspicion was friendly.

"Need to go somewhere," he said. "See the world."

Larry Lee was sleeping couch to couch because his former wife had run him off the plantation three tries into married life. Larry was only too happy to walk two dogs and sleep on Al's fold-out while he "thought things through in the relationship."

"Can't fit 'em all in my car," said Birdsall. "Actually I guess I could. A little cramped, though."

"Take the ground rules. Make out the lineup card. Hit in the four-hole, you want. Let Ivan throw the first game."

"Where you going?"

"L.A. Bring your girlfriend, sit her on somebody's lap."

"Have fun," said Birdsall. "Elizabeth?"

"She's still there, yeah. Ever been?"

"Nope." Loneliness echoed in Birdsall's voice.

"Birdsy, how long you been playing ball with me? So what you're manager one game. They'll listen to you."

"They fucking better."

"Bring your girlfriend."

"Went to Africa. Morocco, anyway."

"Get a new one. She meet a black man, she gone."

Once the plane climbed above the gray-blanket weather over the East Coast, sunlight thundered through the porthole windows the entire flight to L.A. Al's memories of air travel had rusted a bit. Unremembered was the afterlife sensation of a throbbing tube packed with revelation-strength illumination. He felt spiritually pierced by the sun.

His New Yorkness re-asserted itself in Baggage Claim. Large men in Hawaiian shirts hugged sundress-wearing women; surfer-looking kids turned floor-sliding into an Olympic event, and everyone shouted instructions as to where so-and-so was parked. New York airports seemed no different, Al tried telling himself, but then admitted, "I'm on another fucking planet."

In sunlight parallelograms under the Departures overhang

he caught his first glimpse of Los Angeles: samples of Southern California botany and parking garage design. When a green cab popped its trunk, smells of oil rag, spare tire and jerry can of gas evoked a site-specific knowledge.

"So I'm here," he said, shrunken by the newness of his environment, starting with the hotel mattress. "And where is that? Just out of curiosity. 'Here?'"

"Culver City. Why? You don't like it?"

"Let you walk around? Because I don't see nobody."

Elizabeth had answered the phone chanting the name of a real estate company. "Sit tight for an hour. Then I'm off."

They ate that night near what must have been the Pacific Ocean because fog rolled in when they walked back to her car. "What were those called?" he said.

"Mai tais."

"You drive."

"Was going to, anyway. My car, remember?"

Parked near his hotel entrance, she told him how Culver City once boasted movie stars and studios, grand avenues and nice buildings. She had been cagey, though, about exactly where she lived.

"I'm tired," he said. "*You* looking pretty good, though."

"You don't belong out here, hon."

"Don't be saying that, first day."

A few less pounds, a new sassiness which went with a style of haircut Al had not seen before, these changes in her had leaned out at him over the course of dinner.

"Never going back?" he said.

She smiled. "For a visit."

That night, lying on his bed in a blast of outdoor lighting, Al realized what she liked about L.A. Money flowing, big cars, real estate pinballing up and up and up. No old grimness like New York. A sadness smacked him, knowing she was gone for good. Stifling an impulse to fly home, he fell asleep, waking often in the beige darkness to reconfigure his impressions of Los Angeles into a possible docking alignment with himself.

"Not so strange," he said.

"There's familiar stuff. Lots of New Yorkers."

"Biggest assholes out here?"

She laughed. "I have found, yes."

They toured an outdoor mall. Girls staggeringly beautiful at fifty feet seemed unremarkable at five and only sunlight effect on human skin denoted any kind of age. He felt the fatness of her breast as she took his arm, but no memory attached itself to what was briefly physical about her.

"Billboard life," he said.

"Don't knock it."

Finally secure against residual feelings for him, she allowed him to visit her little house. Up a wide sunny street edged with palms they traveled. Up a flagstone path to a shingle-roofed Colonial bungalow chock-a-blocked with what Al imagined to be leftovers from 1950's TV shows. Shiny wooden cuckoo clocks, scalloped shelves, flap-out dowels hinged at the sink to hold dishtowels on.

"Boyfriend?"

"Lot of girls out here get married just to get divorced. Yeah, I do. No hurry, though."

"He like this place?"

She laughed. "It's all mine, Al."

"Beats the fold-out."

"At times, it doesn't." They sat at her formica kitchen table. She took his hands.

"Right here's where I'll remember you," he said, freeing one hand. He tried to look away, not trusting his voice. New York seemed dusty and small to him then. Empty, defenseless, all about the past.

"I can't," he said.

"I know."

Soaring in a cab over the Triboro Bridge, racheting up to his apartment in the metal-clad elevator hoping Larry Lee was ready for his next couch, Al felt his worthless old life slip back over him like a baseball glove.

Without Rebecca to squire to restaurant dinners, Henry's ground shifted towards the pursuit of May Roehmer's commitment to his parking garage. Her office was in a storage dive off Tenth Avenue arrowed through by sprinkler pipes. Gimlet-eyeing him through her cigarette smoke, she rattled on about rumors that the old car barns were being renovated for painter studios and art gallery space. Henry tried listening to what she said in hopes that this *oratorio* was not preamble to her desertion of his project.

"I can get a loan," he said. "If you serve as guarantor."

"I like it when both sides has some risk."

"Do I mind fucking myself just to get this started?"

"Banks don't see it that way, son."

On the way over to her pier shed, May explained grimy industrial Chelsea to him. West of Tenth Avenue was landfill, high tide salting up the underground electrical grid. "Once it's dark," she said, "you walk down this street, middle of the street. Sidewalk's too dangerous. And you don't cross Tenth Avenue somebody's chasing you."

In the desultory stir of river air, Henry wondered who on earth would want to park over here. Under the pier he clocked two probable drug deals and a certain blow job. "Look, you don't have to," he said. Rudely, May hooted. "Don't you ever get hot in that sweater?" He was actually curious.

She frowned. "Thin-blooded."

"Is my desperation coming through?"

"Quit scaring me with how fucking deranged you are. And that scares me, too," she said when he grinned. "You're loosey-goosey enough for ten."

She smoked while Henry went totally present tense, lost in wavelet-slapping sounds. Out of sunstruck chivalry, negotiating the vehicle attack of the West Side Highway, he nearly took her arm. The gesture summed up his despair.

"Two months," she said. "But that's it. I know from the cut of you there's money somewhere. You got two months from the day we open to find an investor, cover your share."

"Really?"

"Don't say, 'really,' just get a line of credit."

In the Bronx Pete McCann was making out his trip sheet in a transit mixer cab. Still in a riverine state, Henry flowed over to him. "Are they up to something?"

"Who?"

"In your judgment."

Pete stared at the trailers. "What are you looking for? Not there. You, yourself?"

"Maybe it's how I grew up. Family-family on the surface. Underneath, all kinds of egregious shit."

"So you're a 'knowledge makes you free' kind of guy?"

"Apart from the pointless stupidity of that, yeah."

Late afternoon smog quilted the blue Bronx air. Sunlight, operating in a mode the reverse of mirage, imposed a painful clarity on every viewable object.

"So what do you end up with?" Pete asked.

"Nothing much. Except you don't depend on illusions to be who you are. Hey, that's pretty good, actually."

From his trip sheet Pete ripped off a scrap, scribbled a number. "Call her," he said.

"Fuck!" Henry realized. "She's *your* cousin, too."

On his couch that evening, phone in his lap, Henry called her. A movie, maybe a bite to eat?

"How about tomorrow night."

"No," he said. "Tonight."

She laughed. "Tonight?"

They met at a midtown theatre. Over the seatback he draped his arm, palming her shoulder. The way she moved into him said nothing of sex and yet did not seem neutral, either. Later, as they ate at a checked-tablecloth Third Avenue cafe, intermittent Rebecca memories speared him in the chest. How he and Nina found themselves on the West Side, kissing on a bench under the sycamores of the Natural History Museum, he could not have reconstructed on a bet.

About his fiancee, he told her this: terrific girl. About herself, she revealed the following: Yorkville, born and bred, art school, then a filmmaking apprenticeship; her father dead, her mother, the sister of Hugh Lynch. Grants kept her afloat, along with work as a camera operator on TV commercials. Breaking up the necking session, she asked, "Do you like your job?"

"Not really. But I like what I want to do."

"That's important," she said.

"You love what you do, don't you?"

"Yes," she said. "But for a man work comes first. Then the wife and kids. It's the only way he can be happy."

"Hey!" On the third iteration of "Hey" Henry realized the voice doing the "hey"-ing was one he knew.

"Hi, girls. Sarah, this is Nina Mortensen. Wait, I fucked that up. Murray. And Cindy, Candy, her girlfriend, friend."

"Hope you're not pretending to be a reporter again."

"What are you kids doing out so late? This woman's a lawyer," Henry said to Nina.

"What part of anything does that explain?" Nina said.

Sarah laughed. Candy appeared dour and Henry knew why. "Where's my regular girlfriend, right?"

"Yes," said Candy. "No offense," she said to Nina.

"His girlfriend's in Morocco," Nina said.

"I remember that now."

"We met through the place Henry works." Connecting Nina with "the place Henry works," Sarah inferred the proper significance. Which left Nina visibly disturbed.

"Sarah's at a fancy law firm," said Henry quickly. "Used to be a prosecutor. My legal advisor."

Sarah and Candy, they had been "caught," too, he realized. Sarah shook Nina's hand. "Enjoyed meeting you."

"Exactly how much legal advice does he need?"

A careful chaffing ensued, featuring Henry, the brave, Henry, the obtuse. Second cousin Dicko never entered the conversation. The couples parted ways.

On Central Park West, they undertook an existential quest

for a cab, perfectly content with a no-cab result. "Listen. Pete, your cousin? Did that actually happen, shooting the little boy?" Henry had no way to gauge this girl. The spiritual tumult she had ignited warred against the recalled thrill of kissing her.

"I don't know," she said. "I never asked him."

"Really? I mean, you're kidding."

Unaware of doing so, they had attracted a cab, its driver the audience for many such partings. Nina allowed Henry to embrace her, then shook his hand. As she was ferried away, he sensed the impermanence of her departure. In the receding rear window of the cab she seemed just another passenger, but he knew very well she was not just another girl.

"Caught them how?"

"What I should have done. Calling the banks. Chemical Bank, Marine Midland. Debiting and crediting hundreds of checks, in different amounts at branches all over the city. He's using the mails, too, which I'm sure has some kind of federal flypaper attached to it."

Locking his hands behind his head, Ray noted the tube of fat money-belting his waist. This led to him pondering the ratio between girth and wealth in the 19th century. The poor populated the sinewy class then. Now stockbrokers banked serious gym-time, pursuing fit and trim, while blue-collar slugs went in for the bisected sandbag look.

"You want to walk and talk this out of the office, Ray? "

"But do they know? The banks."

"About the overdrafts? Which I bet is for millions."

"Do they know?"

"I'm at a loss what to do."

"Why 'at a loss?'"

"Because it's complicated. I'm not even sure it is a kite. Probably it is. Dicko feeding his other companies while he waits for a judgment reversal. You think the fix is in?"

"That *is* troubling."

"I'm hitting Dicko with this. No more memos."

"Wait for the judgment."

"Supposing. Like Sarah said. He's got a federal probe up his ass. What's the moral thing? I'm asking."

"The moral thing? Well, once the ruling's announced..."

"Handed down in September. I suppose I could wait."

Inspired by his close reading of start-up business magazines, Ray had become mildly obsessed with exploring outside-the-box thinking for personal nest egg growth. "Can't do what?" he said, catching the question mark in Henry's voice.

"'Wait.' I can't wait. That's the thing. Not this time."

"Of course not," said Ray, obeying his new business maxim. Run with the river, let the game come to you.

"What?"

"'Let the game come to you.' Why can't you wait?"

"Because," said Henry.

"Where are you going?" Henry had climbed to his feet. "Anyway, keep me abreast. How's your girlfriend, by the way?" Ray called after him. No answer.

At his window Ray guessed "hot ouside," even though the August sky seemed October-ish. Such seasonal mingling put him in mind of interpersonal connections. For instance, Birdsall and Rebecca Van Rijn. Birdsall and Dicko Fitzgerald. Birdsall and Sarah Mortensen. Patterns unnoticed appeared to the unwary as randomness. Closing his eyes, Ray envisioned himself as a hollow tree trunk.

"Nice view," said Drew Case.

Ray looked at his watch. "Why not?"

"Free?"

"Chinese?"

Into the grim cheeriness of the same restaurant on Lexington they plunged again these many months later. "Last time was around Halloween," recalled Ray.

"A gin rickey," said Drew.

The waiter nodded, dealt two menus from his deck.

Drew appeared shrunken to Ray, his features more concentrated in the boat wake of his face, his postage stamp forehead newly re-issued in a reduced size. Age, not stress, had accomplished this. "Know what you're going have?"

"A killing."

"To eat," said Ray.

"What I always have, the duck. You can buy in, too."

"Nice of you. Let's hear it."

"A friend of my son's. Don't ask me how he knows him. Works at a printing outfit downtown. Oaths of silence, all that secrecy stuff. They print the boilerplate for stock offerings, IPOs, proposed mergers. He told my son…"

"You got out, right? When the stock was still high?"

"Do you want to know about this thing, Ray. Yes, I did. To answer your question. Which I find a little inappropriate."

"Suppose I was taping you?"

"Tape recording me?"

"I'm serious."

"You'd make a lousy cop, Ray. Lots of un-incriminating statements. What I was about to say does not fall, legally, under whatever rubric you think it does."

"So a garden variety stock tip then?"

"Quit trying to scare me. What are you looking at?"

Tracking Ray's gaze, Drew swiveled in his chair. Ray now experienced the shudder of prophecy. Across the room, Dicko Fitzgerald to a fanfare of bows and smiles from the serving staff had hurled himself into a chair. Opposite sat Henry Birdsall. The world according to Ray coalesced at this moment.

"Who's the big guy?" said Drew.

"The one with him works for us. It's a bunt."

"A compliance job? Yeah, I remember. Vaguely. Arthur Tannenbaum. Ran into him the other day. Same old, same old, except with Peat Marwick. Anyway, the IPO is for a new cold plate process these people have figured out. Goes on at five bucks. Subscription hasn't even started yet."

In his own mind, Ray had become an astral body capable of multiple attentions. Reading the body language of Birdsall and Dicko, calculating the debt owed him by Drew, Ray floated into a realm of non-verbal sapience. "And?"

"One of the principals wants a membership in my club."

"How many?"

"Monday's the offering. I'm in for a hundred large."

Ray laughed.

"You want me to loan you the dough."

"At what price?"

Drew made a thumb-and-forefinger circle. "As a personal favor, 90-day note." Across the room, Dicko leaned over the table, intent. From this Ray deduced Henry had laid out his findings on the check-kiting scam.

"Fine, then don't take a flyer, Ray, see if I care. Believe me, I'm agnostic here."

"My own money. But thanks. Fifty thousand shares."

That night, Ray rose in the middle of a solo dinner in town to call Dora, eating at home with the girls.

"What's the matter?" she said.

"We can't go into a crouch. Gotta keep punching."

"Are you drunk?"

"I took a risk today."

"That was a mistake."

"Hard to explain."

She sighed. "So you'll explain it to me."

Returned from the pay phone to his steak frites served at the end of the same bar where he had once had a drink with Sarah Mortensen, Ray wondered if another sign from heaven, vis-à-vis Drew's initial public offering, had been Henry Birdsall's guts in confronting Dicko Fitzgerald. Patterns, Ray thought triumphantly. The wisdom of the random.

Perhaps he *was* a little drunk.

Back at his office, Dicko reached into his desk and switched off the tape recorder. "Here's what it is. An unauthorized loan. Thanks to an onerous and unfair judgment. An unauthorized loan, at worst. Hughie, we got Sister Mary Birdsall in our midst."

Hugh Lynch had issued into Dicko's office. "And what could this be about? Not our Chemical Bank deposits, I hope."

"And withdrawals. Same for Midland Marine."

"Marine Midland," corrected Dicko, "get it straight."

"We have every intention of paying the money back."

"Right, 'every intention.' I need a fucking slide rule to keep track. You're covering costs at your other companies with cash from uncredited deposits?"

"You try bonding $10 million sometime. Yeah, it's off," said Dicko to Hugh, whose glance had inquired: tape recorder?

"So sell some companies."

"That's what they want us to do," said Hugh, piously.

"You better do something, or you'll end up in jail."

"Says you," said Hugh. " Says Mr. Henry Birdsall. The one going out with my niece. Mr. Henry Birdsall, the lawyer, is it now? The one who went to a prissy Ivy League school for his business degree. Knows nothing about real business, though. Has a rich girlfriend to marry if business gets too trying for him. Does this help us at all when Dicko and myself try to keep jobs on the table? When we try to create value not just opinions? Does your stiff-necked Protestantism really get us anywhere?"

"Oh, bullshit, Hugh. He's just a kid who grew up soft."

Studying the cousins, Henry remembered a travelogue he had seen once about Ireland. Two men in tweed caps with the guileful humorous faces of goblins. "Well," he said, and his voice shook, "all that might be true. But, Hugh, I understand the breakfast nook in your Catskills house now seats forty-five."

Dicko came around his desk like a bull. "Get the fuck out of this office!" Henry, flinching, stood his ground.

"The banks already know this, Mr. Birdsall."

"Do they? And which one woke up first to find itself holding the bag? And how many checks did you kite?"

Dicko, surprisingly, laughed. "Quite a few."

"How I renovate my kitchen is no concern of yours. Would you like to 'management consult' my tax return?"

Henry suffered a vision of Hugh's niece. His willful moral blindness at Armor Tech must be corrected, yes, but by doing so he had forfeited the Irish girl. "Your tax return. Yeah, that'd reward a look."

"Shaft us again?" said Dicko. "Face the consequences."

At the elevator bank Henry withstood stony looks from the front office gorgons. At the garage a grim little car jockey disappeared with his Fiat keys. In normal protocol a second parker should have time-stamped Henry's ticket stub. Instead, parker number two had vanished, probably on a men's room visit. Up the ramp behind Henry footsteps approached. Other customers, he speculated, just as a sawed-off baseball bat smashed into the side of his head. Wondrously, like a bird uplifting from a treetop, an insight occurred.

Install a toilet in his parking shed.

Henry went fetal as the two men kicked him. Shielding his head, his hands took a hammering from sharp-toed shoes. He heard his nose crack. The big guy in a heave of impressively casual strength reared Henry to his feet. The skinny bat wielder tried for a break shot to the ribs. Henry torqued a jab to the big guy's face, snapping the man's head back and bringing pain to his eyes, but more disquieting, delight. A tremendous uppercut mapped out for Henry the whereabouts of his internal organs. He vomited. Careful to hit as many shoes as he could.

"Motherfucking cocksucker!" screamed the skinny guy.

"And behave yourself," grunted the fat one before swiftly, but in no real hurry, exiting the garage with skinny.

Spanish poured out of the parking attendant when he spotted Henry on the ground. Careening home on auto-pilot,

Henry staggered into his bathroom and urinated blood. In the sink mirror: swollen nose, gashed ear, black eyes. Also, broken knuckles and an odd internal sensation, hopefully not bleeding. Partial thoughts ran through his head, along with a yearning for the Irish girl. Rebecca had written him a letter from Morocco and a post card. In each instance sounding very far away.

Henry decided to cab down to the Lenox Hill Emergency Room. His sweat-soaked underwear when he changed clothes brought back the memory of his lunch with Dicko. During the beatdown the fat mafiosi had said, "Behave yourself." Henry had noticed these two at Cangelosi Concrete. Behave himself about what, the check-kite? How? He had not yet enlightened the banks. Surely the underworld did not work *that* fast.

At the hospital, interns assessed the damage. Bruised kidney, the most serious. Two broken knuckles, a fractured rib. A clean break to the bridge of his nose, therefore a lucky break, and a concussion. They kept him in overnight, releasing him the next afternoon after filing a police report.

"A fight with my cousin," he told an uninterested detective from the 19th Precinct. "Too fucking big, that guy."

"Cousins, yeah, aren't they all? So," said the detective, "charges against this… " he consulted his report for the name Henry had made up, "… Bobby Martin?"

"How about a boxing lesson?"

"No trouble for me to run him in."

Declining his offer, Henry remembered waking up with a shock in the ER hallway, where he had spent the night due to a room shortage. If he left Cross & Case, he would have to buy health insurance. His realization that he had no idea what coverage cost masked a deeper surprise. He was still intending to go out on his own.

When he returned home his phone was ringing.

He let it ring.

Dismay overtook Sarah Mortensen. Intellectually, the challenge of her legal work remained, thank God, but she had begun to re-visit the wisdom of her defection from the criminal justice system. Corporate law lacked *gravitas*.

Candy also depressed her. Although sex with a woman gave her unexpected pleasure, she found herself homesick for a particular type of man. She called Ray Levin.

"Birdsall shit in his hat and put it on."

"Colorful, Ray. How so?"

"No more Baseball for Bonzo, he's got a cast on his hand. Dicko and his people are kiting checks. He confronted them. They had him pulverized."

"Hospital?"

"Not really. So then he went to the banks. I'm wondering. Can we leave this out of our compliance report?"

"What happened with the banks?"

"Dicko got there first. Saying he would pay 'em back. Twenty-three mil when the music stopped. These assholes had kited nine billion dollars worth of checks. Nine billion!"

"Dean's, okay? And bring lover boy."

"That I can't promise."

Hanging up, Sarah leaned back in her leather chair, central air gently jiggling the beaded chains controlling the window blinds. In the framed snapshot on her desk, her brother, Tim, looked handsome and sad. More than once had she been asked was that her husband, but only once had she answered, yes. In the photographed smiles of her parents she imagined she could see strain. The burden of incomprehension revealed itself in the neck cords of her mother, in the false brightness of her father's eyes. They are actually shrieking, she fantasized.

A knock on her door. Candy.

Sarah had arranged to have her assistant/lover shifted to another female lawyer. The strategy, she explained, contained several benefits. Greater cover for their relationship, and for Sarah an eye into the doings of a competitor at the firm.

"Dinner and a movie?"

"Maybe a movie, sweetie. But later. Say, eight."

Candy nodded, happy even in disappointment. Crossing the carpet, she floated onto the desk an inter-office memo. Swung and shimmied her bottom out of the office.

"I want this kid out of harm's way," Ray said to Sarah that evening at Dean's. "No more Lord Jim of the Bronx just because Armor Tech capsized on our watch."

"You don't report the kite and it comes out? You're colluding. That's actionable."

"He told the banks."

"He needs to tell the judge."

Henry Birdsall weaved across the room, face misshapen, bandage wrapping his fist. A *frisson* of disgust rippled through Sarah at the heedlessness of men. They never stopped with the stupidity, the staggering swaggering "determination." For an instant, she missed Candy, her rationality and the ethers of her flesh. "Where's your girlfriend?" she asked Henry.

"Back soon."

"My wife," said Ray, "saw you two in the papers again."

"Yeah, someone said. She's in Morocco."

"So you mentioned," said Sarah.

"Mentioned?" said Ray. "When?"

Indicating his physical condition, Sarah said to Henry, "Put it in your next report." Henry shrugged dismissively. "Why not?" He had stitches in his neck, too.

"See what I mean," said Ray.

A moment later, gulping his drink, Ray exploded into incomprehensibility. While he banged on about a large position he had taken in an IPO, Henry offered up suggestions void of intelligence and Sarah speculated on how long she and Candy might remain a couple. Influenced by the male chest-thumping at the table, she imagined sleeping with other women.

"You're not going back up there," said Ray to Henry.

"Yeah, I am. Tomorrow."

Checking his watch, Ray pushed back his chair. "Make him see reality," he said, pecking Sarah a bourbon kiss.

"Why didn't you?" Sarah said as Ray departed.

"Tell the cops? Because I'm not sure they're connected. The kite and the beating."

"What about the crane accident?"

"Believe me, I'm not making excuses for these Irish pricks. Although they could be, I guess. Connected."

Along with the chill of the amped-up air-conditioning, a profound boredom descended on Sarah. This is why I left, she remembered. The impulse towards evil, endlessly repeated and addressed; the murder trials, prison sentences and plea bargains. At stale moments in her prosecutorial career, these realities had seemed crushingly non-adult, the feckless play of boys.

Outside, Henry tried to magnet a cab from the sparse Tenth Avenue traffic. Sarah stood on the sidewalk.

"I liked that girl," she said.

He lowered his cab-waving arm. "You find one. Another shows up. You can meet people at the wrong time, you know."

"Sure you don't want a ride?"

He shook his head decisively. She got in the cab.

"Don't get mugged," she said as he strode into the shadows of Hell's Kitchen. But she had grasped the connection between this Ivy Leaguer and the thugs she once prosecuted. Whatever they seemed to fear was not what they were actually afraid of.

Lying in bed with Candy, listening to a midnight rain, she put her arm around her sleeping friend and vowed to stay true.

"A little industrial accident," Henry told Al by phone. "No good for Sunday, then?"

"How was L.A.? Also, when does the fall league start? Second question first."

"The fall league? How bad you get hurt."

"Knuckles mostly. And a rib. My mitt hand, though. I'll need a couple weeks."

"What'd you do? Get in a fight?"

"Listen, I'll be out there soon. Just not Sunday. Or the next couple of."

"You need anything or anything?"

Henry glanced around himself. Panic boiled up in his throat at the thought of growing old in this room. "I'm fine."

At Fitzgerald Sand & Stone, Henry parked his Fiat in the sun-crisped weeds and crossed towards the trailers, utterly null to suspense over what his reception would be.

"Well, if it isn't himself, come to grace us with his presence," said office manager, Rollo McIntyre. "I'm amazed you'd show your face."

Henry headed for his desk, trailed by hard looks.

"Asshole."

"Tattletale."

"Tell me you hit the man back, for God's sake!"

"Two of them, and yes, I did, Karen, not that it helped."

"You put our jobs in jeopardy."

"By the way, Angie. It's your people who thugged me."

"They should have done a better job."

As the morning progressed, however, Henry realized style points had been granted him for having dared come to work. Obscenely insincere, Frank and Jackie offered to wreak vengeance on his behalf. "They use knucks?" asked Jackie.

"You must bruise something fierce," said Frank.

"Sawed-off bat. The kind bartenders use."

"Maybe they *were* bartenders."

"The way it works, Frank," said Henry, "is you can't just take money from a bank, they have to give it to you."

"Must tell father."

"I think father already knows," Jackie said.

"Fucks it up with your girlfriend, though, Hugh's niece. I'm sure you've gone crying to the judge as well."

"And what do you think happens if he's in their pocket?"

"You betrayed us."

"Betrayed *you?*" Henry exclaimed. "'Let's go bouncing?' A clamshell drops on my head. 'Hey, here's my cousin.' I get the shit beat out of me. You played me like a fucking… what's that Irish instrument?"

"Piccolo," said Jackie. Frank stared at him.

"Harp. What do you mean, 'piccolo?'"

Jackie's eyes married-up, his chest swelling. The tension had broken. As he headed across the workyard, even Henry was laughing. "Still, you fucked us," Frank yelled after him.

In the second trailer, Christine Dicker took Henry aside. "You think we weren't exhausted, writing all those checks? The depositing, I'll miss. You could plead traffic if you slagged off part of the day."

"Thank you."

"For what? You're not to tell a soul what I said."

Molly gave him a waspish, disappointed look. "We'll watch for the announcement in the papers, Henry. Tell all our friends we know a famous groom."

"They're not going to jail, okay."

"Oh, but I heard they were," she said, innocently.

"Nothing that dramatic."

"Just imagine. Her uncle, Hugh, the husband of her mother's sister, Maeve. And Dicko, her second cousin. Maybe she can make a documentary about it."

Outside, Henry ran into Pete McCann, back from a bombing run to a midtown job site. Pressure-hosing concrete detritus off the carriage of his transit mixer, Pete flicked the nozzle closed. Instead of speaking, Henry shrugged.

"They're not as pissed off as they look," said Pete. "Dicko turns up his toes on this? So what? They'll all find other jobs. It just won't be family."

"What kind of shit am I standing in?"

Training the compressed jet on midget asteroids of smut, Pete peeled nubbins of concrete off the scarred metal. When he smiled Henry saw his tiny dingy Irish teeth. "Whatever it is, you'll figure it out."

That night, at the Market Diner on Eleventh Avenue, Henry met with May Roehmer during her dinner hour. "You're spoiling my meal," she said as Henry sat down.

"I warned you."

"Yeah, but over the phone. Over the phone I can't see you. By the way, get used to this. You know, don't you, who'll be sniffing around us?"

"Why? Because all-cash?"

"You stand up to these greaseballs is the only way."

"Here's what we need. A toilet for the parkers."

May laughed. "When'd that come to you?"

"Middle of getting my head beat in."

"And the check, honey. New girl," she said to Henry, indicating the waitress. "Thank you," she said a moment later. She then re-ran the woman's addition with a carpenter pencil before slapping down bills and change,.

Henry glanced at the check. "I think you stiffed her."

May glared at him. The waitress approached. Still pretty beneath a netting of facial lines, she assessed by touch the exact dollar amount. Paused, then frowned.

"Tip's in there, honey," said May.

The waitress stared at the check. At May. "I'll alert Chase Manhattan," she said, moving away.

"Ow," said Henry, laughing. "That makes my ribs hurt. You left her twenty-five cents, for Christ's sake."

"I'm gonna need you full time," May said outside in the parking strip, "so start practicing your goodbyes. And you got money to raise. Don't forget."

From a phone booth, Henry called Nina. Exhaustion chewed on his resolve. "Can I talk to you about something?"

"Okay," she said. A lightness, even delight, in her voice

"We could do it tomorrow."

"Sure. If you want."

"Or now. I'm in a phone booth."

"Not on my corner, I hope."

They met in front of her building and walked towards Gramercy Park. Her response to his discolored face did nothing to diminish his sense of her as coolly empathetic. She did not care, she said, what Henry had done to jeopardize the finances of her uncle and second cousin. Did not care whether his actions meant incarceration for them both.

"What about your mother?" he asked nervously.

"I don't think that'll be a problem." She laughed. "Not really a problem, no." She glanced at him. "Were they the ones did this?" What he liked was how uninflected she was. No false sentiment lurked behind her statements.

"Somebody did," he said.

They had circled back to her building. She wanted him to come up. Desperately, he wanted to come up, too. With superhuman effort neither would allow this. So they said goodnight and Henry went home.

Roughing out the dreaded conversation on the flight back from Casablanca, Rebecca found Henry's dialogue easier to imagine than her own. While dining with Sally and Ben Maxwell at a private-home restaurant in Tangiers, the words "way too early" had popped into her consciousness. The subtly violent shock of being in a foreign country had amplified the voice in her head. Way too early, she understood, to salt herself away in marriage.

"What's the big hurry?" Sally Maxwell asked. "You think for a moment he won't stick around? If he doesn't, there's others, trust me. Get out and about before making the jump. Because unless you get divorced, you're in for a very long cruise. Nothing wrong with that, of course. Divorce."

"Do you ever miss the States?"

Sally laughed. "A friend of ours, Aaron Hecker, based in Cairo. You know, on-air ABC? Got promoted and married. I asked him how he liked it. 'Fine,' he said. 'Except I hate my new job and I miss dating.' That's not exactly Ben and I, as far as Tangiers, but we wish we were back sometimes, yes."

"That's helpful, actually."

"You can do anything you want, Becca. So go do it!"

Driving with the Maxwells through the Anti-Atlas to Marrakech, Rebecca kept looking forward to her apartment share on the Upper West Side and to her first non-scholastic autumn since kindergarten. The Maxwells had booked them into the Mamounia Hotel. Arriving at night with the french doors open to the fragrance of orange blossoms, she was ovewhelmed with remorse. Morning revealed out her window the *orangerie* source of her sensory overflow. She called Henry long distance. No answer, the operator said.

That afternoon at a rendezvous with Mark in the Djema el Fnaa, the central square of Marrakech vivid with water carriers, snake-sellers and other implausible actors performing the word "exotic," she felt like a freshman visiting a friend at another college. On a balcony above the square, leaning over his glass of tea, Mark bowled her over with a single remembered gesture: the clawing back of a lock of his hair.

A day later they smoked hashish together. The impetus for her intention to sleep with Mark lay largely in her newfound belief that the lives of married people should be privately lived. Straddling him in the torpid heat of late afternoon, she spotted through the reed shade over his window chickens observing her from an adjoining roof. Her pleasure at being monitored in a carnal moment by members of the animal kingdom confirmed her new reluctance to rush into a choice of mate. She slept with Mark twice more before returning with the Maxwells to Tangiers.

"So a good time was had by all," said Ben, on the drive back through the mountains.

Prone on the back seat, enduring a stomach bug, Rebecca caught the look Sally shot her husband. Not to answer was to answer, so she said, "Well, *I* had fun."

"This was good for you," said Sally.

"What about you two?" Rebecca asked, tamping down with her palm an embarrassing stomach gurgle.

"We had fun," said Ben, matter-of-factly.

An hour further on while squatting in ceramic footprints over a vile cesspit in a spectacularly fetid toilet stall, Rebecca rolled up her entire three days with Mark in Marrakech, snapped a rubber band over the experience and filed it away as the first of what she hoped her near future would bring. After which, grown sexually wise and replete, she would return to Henry and get married.

As her flight descended into Kennedy she decided to seek counsel from her aunts. After three weeks of disorienting events, she yearned for the amniotic fluid of kin. Henry would have to wait.

"Liked all those postcards," said Diana.

"I was busy."

"Did you write grandmother. Or at least call her."

"That reminds me," said Rebecca, heaving up from the patio table. Since the wheels of her plane had touched down, she had barely given Henry a thought. Lumped on a stool in the pantry, she now returned his call.

"They said you went straight to Southhampton."

"Who did? Harriet?"

"Your grandfather. What's he doing, anyway, answering the phone?"

"Yeah, I'm here," she said.

"You want me to drive out?"

"Monday, I'll be back."

"Monday."

"Come out if you want. But you don't have to."

"My car's in the shop. I guess I could take the jitney."

"Or you could take the train."

"I could."

"If you wanted to. But I'll be back Monday."

From this, they moved on to her trip, although both voices struggled to hide a self-protective lack of interest in what the other had been up to. Yes, Morocco was interesting. What about him? Certainly, he missed her, he said.

"How's your friend," she managed to say.

"How's yours," he returned sharply.

"He's good. Has she gone back to Nicaragua yet?"

"Not yet. So I guess I'll see you when you come back."

"Call you soon as I get in."

"I love you."

"Me, too. I mean, you, too."

Rebecca felt fragmented. Part of her was drawn by Henry's voice to the physical memory of him. Part of her was embarrassed by having nearly had to say in front of Patty, the cook, the three big words, which even more distressingly she was no longer sure she felt. And, finally, part of her was annoyed by the strain in *his* voice when he said, "I love you."

Back out on the patio, Diana was reading a novel and Laura meditatively sipping ice tea. Rebecca emerged, drained but resolute. Diana looked up at her. "Is he coming?"

Unprepared to answer that, she sat down.

"Is Bo in there?" asked Laura.

Rebecca shrugged. Laura abandoned the patio for the kitchen. Diana watched her leave. Turned to her niece, raised an eyebrow. "I just thought it would easier," Rebecca said.

"Without him."

Rebecca switched into a defensive mode. "He's fine. He wanted to come out. We just thought, wait until after the weekend. He's got work to do and stuff."

Diana succeeded in appearing not to assign significance to this development, but Rebecca suspected first causes had been noted in love's decline. "And this is nice," Rebecca said. "End of summer." She gestured at the heat-fatigued trees, their leaves torqued to silver undersides; the slightly browning lawn. "You know, being here."

"Did you have fun over there."

"I did," she said, assertively.

enry tried not to confront what he knew. That Rebecca's feelings towards him had changed, that he was pressuring her, that she was too young, that he was the wrong one, etc. "This thing has caught me sideways," he told Bobbie over the phone.

"Ride it out," she said, bored.

"I'm serious. I'm ready, she isn't. She's pulling back."

"For now."

"You're not listening. For good."

"Then go out there. And try not to be so dramatic."

That Saturday morning when Ray Levin called with a first time ever invitation to his summer house, Henry saw a positive omen: I will be closer to Rebecca.

"You can hop over on the ferry," said Ray as he drove Henry from the train station, "be there Sunday. A little overcast now, but the beach'll be perfect this afternoon. Dora's looking forward seeing you again. How's everything going?"

"Not so good. But, basically, good."

The shingled summer house smelled of ocean damp and the presentiment of winter. Ray's little girls had friends over, confusing the issue of parentage, as none of the tiny budding females appeared related to each other, or to Ray and Dora.

Henry excused himself, found a phone and dialed.

At the sound of the first ring, he relaxed. Diana, her aunt, answered. "Oh, Henry," she said. "She'll have to call you back. They went into the village. Say, an hour or so?"

"Sure. Tell her I'm just across the Sound."

"Really? Where?"

"Old Saybrook," he said, suddenly mortified.

"That's not exactly right across. Are you coming over?"

"I could. I might."

"Well, you two decide," she said.

During lunch, unnerved by the prospect of hearing what he expected to hear, Henry decided not to phone Rebecca back.

"Let's slow down a little," she said when he did call finally.

"Yeah," he said. "Okay."

"I'll see you when I get back to the city."

"Sure. Say 'hi,' to everyone for me."

"They asked about you."

He declined to be mollified.

Earlier, as Henry slogged across the sand, his ears buzzed with embarrassment. Here he was at thirty, an emotionally embalmed mummy, complete with flapping gauze bandage on his hand. Although protective of him, Ray and Dora did not shrink from presenting themselves as affectively whole. Into the surf they splashed, unafraid to flaunt their suitability for each other. Walking back up from the beach, they held hands. Skittering ahead, the covey of little girls exhibited in shy glances the awareness of a durable event taking place. Despite his humiliating obviousness Henry felt restored.

"It'll happen," said Ray.

"I've pushed at this for so long, but it won't move."

"It's out there for you," Dora said, "somewhere."

They were sitting in the sand-crunchy living room, Henry talking in a subdued voice about how fundamental the idea of marriage was to his sense of who he was. The courtship stories of Ray and Dora hewed to a central theme: each knowing the other was the "right one." Ray telling Dora this two dates into the relationship, Dora taking longer to make up her mind.

"Which is typical," said Ray.

"Not necessarily. You just seemed so sure."

"When you want it bad enough."

"No," said Dora. "You have to be lucky."

"Yes," said Henry, fervently, his thoughts turning to Nina Murray. To envisioning her as a person *like* the one he would end up with. Yes, someone like her. The Irish girl.

Nevertheless, returning to the city Sunday afternoon, he made the decision to wait Rebecca out. He took Monday off, alerting Karen Mulroney in the Bronx, who seemed relieved.

"I imagine you won't be here on Friday either," she said.

"When the judgment comes down? Yeah, I will."

"Fiddlesticks!"

"Possibly. Although I think you mean, 'Bullshit!'"

Late on a beautiful fall morning, caught up in the drama of what he was about to do, Henry called the Park Avenue apartment. Rebecca had returned from Southhampton Monday night. Harriet answered the phone.

"*Henri? Un moment*, please,"

Henry closed his eyes, breathed deeply. On the other end of the line, footsteps approached. A clunk as the phone was picked up.

"Hi," he said, absurdly hopeful.

"Hi," said Rebecca.

After Los Angeles, Al began to more actively consider his political career.

"So what do I need to do?" he asked.

"Raise money," said Rickshaw Reynolds, an advisor to the Borough Democratic Party. "Which means you got to promise things. You the promising type, Al?"

"Ready to do what's necessary. That type."

"Good," said Rickshaw, a mountainous man perpetually renovating a brownstone on Manhattan Avenue. Rearing back from the table, he speared the check from the waiter. "You can start here," he said, handing the check to Al.

"Have some of my own, you know. Money."

"Whatever you do," said Rickshaw, "and I'm serious about this. Don't spend any running for office. Meantime, set you up with some people watching you. Downtown people."

Outside the restaurant, a Peruvian place on Amsterdam, Rickshaw ignited a foul-smelling stogey and extemporized in his mouth-breather voice on Al's chances of winning a City Council seat. The local incumbent, a well-known Upper West Side *La Pasionaria*, observantly Jewish-liberal, had practically declared for mayor. Endless years of Ed Koch had turned up the dial on racial disgruntlement and solid black candidates offered a jittery electorate pressure abatement. "Or so I see it, anyhow," said Rickshaw. "But I'm a lawyer, I can afford to be sang-u-ine. Call me tomorrow, you still serious." Into the faulty darkness he then lumbered after a world-embracing shrug.

Back in his apartment, attended by his audience of dogs, Al kicked off his new career with a phone call. "Who you know might give to a political campaign?"

A throat clearing. "Political campaign?"

"Tell me you not sleeping, 8:30 at night."

"Of course not," said Birdsall. "Let me think. Wait, I got

it. Yeah, this is a great idea."

Two days later, in his midtown office, Birdsall produced Ms. High-Powered Attorney. Al wore a turtleneck and a velour jacket with leather elbow patches. In breezed the lady lawyer, her pinstriped business suit unable to hide the fullness of her upper half. A second female, in gabardine, accompanied her.

"Any other backers?" asked the lawyer, Sarah Mortensen.

"New York State Assemblyman Harrison Fultz. Roy Manton from Harlem. I am tight with my district DC and..."

"Democratic Club," explained the lawyer to her paralegal.

"... there's downtown interest. Rickshaw Reynolds."

"Of course. In a primary who'd you be up against?"

"The field is forming right now," Henry volunteered.

"Birdsall." In the door poked a large head: standard white, Mediterranean tint. Henry heaved to his feet and left. "I'll need this place back in an hour," said the head, grinning suggestively at the lawyer and paralegal.

"Knew Birdsy didn't have no office like this" said Al.

"What was that about?" said the paralegal.

"The appeal," said the lawyer. "Today's the fifteenth."

"What am I missing here?" said Al.

"Have you assembled an organization?"

"Campaign manager went to California, but I got my eye out. I'm in the 'exploratory stages.' Assessing my likelihoods."

"Any polling?"

"Won Community Board by six points."

"What do you think your chances are for Council?"

"You gonna tell me I can't be considered?"

"I live in your district. We both do," the lawyer added.

"Makes it personal, then." Al caught a look between lawyer and paralegal. "We all in this together. Know what I'm saying? Different types, races. Behind the right ideas. Schools, cops, opportunity."

She laughed. "Yeah, keep it vague, whatever you do."

"I'm a guy considers all sides. But I know what it's like to take what they won't give you." He hoped his racial identity made it clear that he grasped what they, too, faced.

"Local politics needs to *include*," said the paralegal.

Al could see that the lawyer wanted to smile and only professionalism kept her from doing so. This, though, was why she had brought her girlfriend along.

"Yes, it does," he said. "Every type under the rainbow."

Exiting the office, they passed a conference room occupied by three men: the Mediterranean guy, a non-Jewish-looking Jew, and Birdsall, obviously the subordinate of the other two, except that Henry was the one on the phone.

"We'll talk again," said the lawyer.

The driver of the Lincoln Town Car held the back door open for her. The paralegal scooted around to the other side. A sensation close to excitement overcame Al as he headed for the subway. A lone wolf he might be, but not one completely outside the cast of campfire light.

"Your friends left," said Freddy Habyan.

"What friends?" said Ray.

"The short one, Henry?"

"They're both short."

"Don't make me say it."

"Large-breasted, Freddy? The lawyer?"

Freddy sat down in a conference room chair, so Ray sat down, too. "Postponement of the Fitzgerald judgment does not close down the gig. Forget why this judge is stalling. They've gotten to him. Right, Ray? Yeah, probably, they have."

"I talked to Legal. Technically, we're still bound."

"It's like *Brigadoon*," said Henry, clutching his brow.

"Why? Your song's over, you're back in the chorus."

"No, next time, they'll kill him," said Ray.

Henry looked up. "Unconnected, the beating."

"Which you don't know."

"He can't be hoping for fresh indictments," Henry said.

"Hoping, who?" said Freddy.

"The judge. So his ass is covered he grants the appeal."

"The papers'd kill him," said Ray. "And the D.A."

"Ray, look at me. Did you write up Birdsall's Bat Day?"

"I begged you not to, Ray," said Henry.

"I don't know which of you assholes is worse. I'm under a lot of pressure here for various fucking reasons which you have no idea of. I don't need this extra shit."

"You sure made 'em happy up at the Raccoon Lodge."

"Who'd you tell?" asked Freddy.

"Henry, you're off the case. Who'd I tell? The clerk for this crooked judge. He goes, 'I'll pass it on to His Honor.'"

"We made a decision, Ray."

Henry stood up. "That explains the postponement."

"What are you involved in now?" said Freddy.

"What?"

"No more favors, okay? You did one already."

While Henry tried to puzzle out the "favor" reference, Ray capsized into woefulness. "I took a big position in an IPO currently headed straight for the south pole," he said.

"Let me guess," said Freddy.

"Don't. That son of a bitch!"

On his way to the Bronx, Henry decided his only human function was decorative. He served ornament not structure. To putter about and procreate summed up his life's purpose. Suicide first, he vowed.

"So did you sleep with him?" he had asked Rebecca finally.

"Did I?" To her credit, she did not mention the Irish girl. "Yes, I did." When Henry hung up, he did so with one finger on the disconnect button, the other dialing Nina Murray.

"Rebecca and I broke up."

"I'm sorry to hear that."

"Could we go out to dinner?"

"Really," she said. "I am."

Crossing the Bronx workyard, Henry's eyeballs bounced from the thud of his heels. Bizarrely short of breath he climbed the wooden steps. As he opened the trailer door the source of his terror made itself known. Nina Murray. From the frying pan with Rebecca he had jumped into the fire.

"We're closing down," said Rollo McIntyre.

"I see Karen's coat," said Henry, nonsensically.

"Good boy," responded Rollo, snapping his briefcase shut. "Shows how observant you are. She only leaves it there every night. In case the a/c gets too frosty during the day."

"For good? Closed."

At the door Rollo said, "You'd like that, wouldn't you?"

Henry now saw the rubber dog turd on his chair. Saw his taped-shut desk drawers and broken pencils. The ringing of two telephones, one after the other, pierced his self-pity.

"Looking for Dicko," said the voice of Russ Cangelosi. "No answer at the office, thought he might be up there."

"Can I ask you something? Maybe come by?"

Dropping over the Throgs Neck into Queens, Henry flexed his right fist, wondering if that hand could yet be admitted to a baseball glove. Beneath the bridge sailboats revealed themselves as divots in the otherwise unmarred ceramic of Long Island Sound. Featureless apartment blocks draped with *Now Renting* flags assumed a sobbing sentimentality as milieu. Along the fence at Cangelosi Concrete, in the misty sunlight of Jamaica Bay, polka-dotted transit mixers lined up like hippos in ballerina skirts. Crossing the workyard, Henry reflected passionately, I love this world.

"Sausage and peppers," said Russ Cangelosi to his secretary as she gathered her purse. "But this time tell him bread's gotta be fresh. Sit down," he said to Henry. "You know how come, don't you? The beating?"

"Generally, yes. Specifically, no."

"I'm out of business, I come in high. Out of business, I don't nail this contract. I called Dicko thinking maybe he could buy me out."

"And those guys thought what?"

"That you had it figured."

"Bid rigging?"

"You got it, champ."

"How come you're telling me?"

"Because maybe there's someone you could tell."

"Fucking Dicko. So it wasn't him."

"Here's what's wiggy. It's you they light up not me."

"Because they know you won't testify."

"I'm talking to you, right? So that's what they want. You see what I'm saying? For some fucking reason, they *want* the ballgame exposed. The Gambinos do. So, the question is, 'Do you know anyone?'"

"First, okay? How does it work?"

"They orchestrate bids. We all come in high. Whoever they control, wins. It's going on in window contracts, too."

"Rumors of a federal probe."

"I heard 'em. I'm using you, kid, don't mistake it."

"I'm *supposed* to be talking is why I got creamed? Fuck

them, I'm keeping my mouth shut."

Cangelosi looked up. "You told him?"

"Right out of the oven, the bread," said his secretary, ferrying over the white paper bag. "Napkins're in there."

Cangelosi extracted his sausage and peppers on a roll. "Go eat some Irish food," he said to Henry. "And tell Dicko to fuck himself. No," he reconsidered, "give him my best, like always."

Climbing in his Fiat, Henry wondered why this watershed moment in his life did not feel more momentous.

At dinner that night with Nina Murray desire turned Henry spastic. Into his lap he knocked a goblet of strawberries and whipped cream.

"Great," he said, wiping himself off.

Nina laughed. "Maybe you need to calm down."

An hour after visiting Russ Cangelosi Henry pulled into the driveway of Dicko's mansion in Rye. Dicko's wife and daughter had just exited the house. The little girl, a sullen perfect beauty, glared at Henry.

"I'd advise you not to go in," Sharon said.

An aged brown woman in a maid's uniform answered the door, Dicko's voice audible from upstairs. "He sung," the maid explained.

Henry nodded. "What's the boy's name?"

"He name Brendan."

Henry went upstairs. In brute impatience Dicko stood on the locked-out side of a heavy-looking door. "Give me a hug, Brendan, for Christ's sake. It isn't gonna kill you."

"What am I gonna do, Daddy?" bleated the boy's voice.

"Goddamnit! I told you. Your mother'll be in charge. Look, it's not very likely I'll be... what the hell!"

"I came by to wish you luck. The engagement's done. You know, the compliance job?"

"I know what an engagement is. Done why? Because you've done all the damage you could?" Turning to the door, Dicko spoke to the presumed curiosity of his son. "Guess who's out here? Same guy who got Daddy in trouble."

"No, he isn't," said the boy's muffled voice.

"Yes, he is." Noting now the faded bruises on Henry's face, Dicko grunted out a laugh. "What happened? You fall down? Jesus, Brendan, come on out. You'll enjoy this. Somebody beat the crap out of the guy."

The door opened. A thin-faced roughneck emerged into the hallway. The bulkiness of his young body struggled for dominance against the woundedness of his eyes. From a distance he viewed Henry's bruises. He laughed, then became somber. "Will that happen to you?" he asked his father.

"I'm not going to jail. And if I do, it won't. I'm too big. Which you'll be, too, once you quit hiding behind doors."

"Listen to your Dad."

"Leave him alone. He's upset."

Walking Henry out to his car, Dicko revealed that Marine Midland and Chemical had filed criminal charges on the check kite. Any postponement whatsoever, Dicko felt, augured badly for the price fixing appeal. "Look, I said nothing about the assault," Henry said. "But if you don't believe me, don't."

"I don't," said Dicko.

Henry could not tell whether Dicko knew about the federal probe. Mainly, he seemed at sea over recent domestic events. "I'll miss it," said Dicko, staring at his mansion. "If it comes to that. Which it won't."

"I don't say it will. But prison might be a relief."

Dicko turned to Henry, the cartoon "Dicko" briefly unavailable as persona. "You ever have trouble with your Dad?" Wanting to say yes, Henry realized that he and Buster rarely even argued. He said yes, anyway. At last glimpse Dicko stood staring up at a small bird trapped in the ivy that spidered in from the corners of his house.

"Just for the record," he said to Nina Murray as they crossed against the light on Park Avenue South, "it wasn't your relatives who had this done." He indicated his face.

"I'm going to miss all that yellow and blue."

"Convince me again your mother won't be upset if her brother-in-law goes down the chute?"

"She won't be. Who was it, then?"

"That's another story."

Bored with his own saga, Henry had caught in her voice the sanguinity of her experiences. She was engaged by his troubles in an eye-on-the-horizon way. Without saying so, she had seen much worse in her life, which freed him, congenially, from his own self-involvement. As they walked home along a sidewalk stencilled with rain felled leaves, she asked had he seen news accounts of an American pilot shot down by Sandinistas. "Running guns to the Contras, of course. But this time a little more overtly."

"Overtly?"

She blinked at his political duncehood, annoyed. "Hired by the C.I.A, he says."

Henry recovered. "I hope no one's surprised."

At the door of her building, she turned and shook his hand. Having expected an invitation to come upstairs, Henry went goggle-eyed. "Thank you for dinner," she said.

"I'm a free agent," he responded, eager as a Shriner.

"I feel badly about it not working out with Rebecca. I'm glad, though, that you and I can be friends." With a suddenness that suggested teleportation, she vanished into her vestibule.

"So you can see for yourself," she said to Henry two nights later in a cab. "How she feels about her brother-in-law."

"Yeah, but really. Why are you doing this?"

"Just ask her. I know you don't believe me."

"There has to be another reason," he said.

The muzzy backseat light of the cab, vaguely, the avenue they were on: Henry would remember these specifics because of what she said next.

"Henry."

"Speaking."

"You need to understand something. With me, it doesn't have to be complicated. You don't have think I'm saying the opposite of what I feel."

Her mother, Regina, lived in a walk-up two-bedroom in a Yorkville tenement. They stood in the kitchen, Regina in a silk pattern office dress. She worked as a private secretary for an industrialist active in philanthropic affairs. "Hughie?," she said. "A greedy, sanctimonious thief, if I'm not being too harsh."

Henry laughed. "Jesus, Regina, speak up."

"And the other one, Richie? Imagine not murdering people calling you 'Dicko?' In fact, insisting on 'Dicko.' He's been naughty since childhood. Although I do feel for him somewhat. That father!"

"What about Hugh's kids?" Henry asked.

"My sister did the best she could. They have slivers of her in them. They're your cousins, Nina. Say something"

"I've had my ups and downs with them. But Daddy tried never to talk about us to each other."

"Shall we go back out," said Regina, indicating the living room, "or have it here in the kitchen? Here, then," she said. "Nina, could you bring in the tea things?"

As Nina slipped from the room, Regina cocked her head at Henry. Shrewdness and rebellion glinted in her marble blue eyes. In the fineness of her throat, Henry predicted an elderly loveliness for her daughter. "Her father was right, of course. Talking about the family. But I do worry for Maeve. Thank you, dear," she said to Nina, who as they seated themselves at the kitchen table molded her hand to her mother's shoulder, a gesture of affection received with an infinitesimal watering of Regina's eyes.

Dancing with Nina to a live band in a Village bar that had succumbed to the country music craze, Henry pendulum-ed from delight to anxiety. Nina bumped and rocked against him in rhythms separate from his own. His pasted-on smile fell off. And then a calm descended. He would not have to pretend with her. She had spoken the truth about herself in the cab.

Later they necked on her couch. Plainly but serenely furnished, her apartment was otherwise a jumble of film cans and equipment trunks. The transaction, which included the transit to her bed, was characterized by a firm desire to yield. As he lowered himself onto her, amazed at the slightness of her shoulders, he experienced, even before entering her, a sense of destination achieved.

"I know you're about to announce. You better be."

"You don't work here, Sarah."

"Oh, really? Well, sorry to rub it in."

"That's funny, actually."

"I don't need which families, Herb. Just the civilians."

"Sarah, I gotta hang up. Rudy just came in."

"Put him on," she said.

The acoustics changed, and then Herb Mauskopf picked up the phone again. "Quit crawling up my ass, okay? Now give me a name. One name. No answer is an answer."

"Ever see *All the President's Men*? Answer/no answer is how they nearly blew the whole scoop. One name it is then. Richard Fitzgerald and Hugh Lynch."

"You're an asshole, you know that."

Sarah laughed. "Does that count as an answer?"

With a friendly snort Herb Mauskopf hung up. They had worked together for Bob Abrams as State AAG's. Sarah leaned into her intercom. "Henry Birdsall, Cross & Case."

"Yes, ma'am. I mean Miss... Morgen, morten..." New secretary. "... sen. Sarah, I mean."

As she waited to be connected to Henry, Sarah toyed with the idea of bringing Candy to Myron and Eve Kandel's next dinner party. Myron, she suspected, held no illusions about Sarah's lack of interest in men.

"Sarah. Miss Morton... son, sen."

Sarah punched the phone off speaker. "Henry?"

"No, it's me," said the secretary. "He's no longer at Cross & Case. They gave me another number for him. I have a May Roehmer on the line."

"Who the hell is she?"

"His new superior, I'm gathering."

The comedy soon became tedious of establishing who was

who and how connected to Henry. "Not working *for* me, goddamnit!" said the woman. "*With* me. We're partners. Or will be, this kid raises his share of the dough."

"Where is he?"

"I'm in the office, for Christ's sake," she said. "Which means he's down at the pier. We open in a week. Ever deal with contractors? Your name's Sarah, right? That's biblical, so you're Jewish? Not that it matters. Getting back to contractors, I'm the one should be taking care of this. Men just fuck it up. They're only good for screaming at people, which he better be doing now."

"I had work done on my apartment."

"Then you know," said May Roehmer, satisfied.

When Sarah hung up, she called Ray. "What on earth?"

"Have you seen him lately? He's totally stressed-out. I still have his severance check."

"A parking garage, Ray?"

"This is some bozo idea he's apparently had forever."

"What happened to the compliance job?"

"We took a waiver. Why?"

"But you're all buttoned up on this?"

"Oh, God! Are we gonna be in the news again? I can't take it, Sarah. Meet me for a drink. Would you? Please."

"Where's his parking garage?"

Not in the mood for Henry's crisis-magnet personality, Sarah had avoided returning his call yesterday. To make up for that, she had milked Herb Mauskopf, a federal prosecutor in the Southern District who, months ago, had let drop word of a racketeering probe into the concrete industry. "I'm supposed to meet your former boss for a drink," she said to Henry now.

"That reminds me. *His* boss has a crush on you."

"I can't tell you how unexcited I am."

"Yes, you can. I'll go anywhere you want, but not with Ray. And not for why you're thinking. He's a good guy."

She met Henry at his parking garage on a West Chelsea pier. "We needed to wire and plumb," he said, giving her the tour. "Throw up some sheetrock for a toilet. Hear the river slapping underneath?"

"Could this be any more desolate?"

"No," he said glumly.

Outside, welders re-beaded ancient pier footings to the shed. A changing wind twinkled over the river from the New Jersey. Mid-September light. Sarah felt old.

"Have to be a little wary down here, especially at night," Henry said as they headed for Tenth Avenue. "Let's cross over and hope they don't follow us." Three bearded men squatting in a doorway watched a tall shirtless man track Sarah and Henry down the street. "So from a guy in a position to know," continued Henry, "I hear about what's called a 'ballgame.' By the way, these vendors are clued-in about that federal probe. Let's cross back over here, under these lights."

"It's now indictments. Racketeering, which means RICO."

The three bearded men had joined the hunting party.

"So union payoffs. Extortion."

"And bid-rigging. Henry, do you really think," Sarah said wearily, "I've never heard the term ballgame before?"

"It wasn't Dicko who had me beat up. Keep moving."

"Too bad. Because he's in the team picture."

At a gas station on Tenth the pursuing zombies evanesced into wraiths. "Thanks for coming down, Sarah. Really."

Up the avenue she zoomed in a cab to an Alsatian bistro on West 54th where she and Ray had agreed to meet, both having admitted to a permanent weariness with Dean's.

"It's dying," said Ray.

"You mean changing. That neighborhood."

"Same difference," he said. "And I'm quits with the whole local-color bit. I just want a city where people are nice to each other, pick up after themselves and don't talk too loud."

They drank bourbon and ate *celeri remoulade*. The ambience consisted of mounted deer heads, uncomfortable chairs and rueful older waiters who seemed to have been college professors once. Maybe the lurking seasonal change veered her thoughts this way, but Sarah sensed discontinuations in her routine.

"I'm finding it hard to get on top of myself," said Ray

"How so?"

"I took a terrific beating. And I hope and presume Drew Case took one, too. I'll pay less income tax, mortgage the house, feel like a jerk for upsetting Dora. But I can wish, can't I, for another kind of world besides this one?"

"Yes," she said, oddly moved.

"So I assume what you avoided referring to over the phone is that federal thing. Anyway, the check kite's a push. Birdsall forced Dicko's hand."

"Can we not talk about this," said Sarah suddenly. "I'm in a change-makes-me-sad kind of mood. You're a provider, Ray, to your wife and kids. That's all that counts."

"So are you. Minus the wife and kids." She smiled. He glanced around the restaurant. "We'll stay friends."

"Phone friends, now that Dean's is done."

He let her leave first, like they had taken a room together, and a few hours later she accused Candy of using her work on that scarecrow black guy's political campaign as a way to meet men. Candy fired back "jealous," "suffocating" and "self-involved." That night, in restive half-sleep, Sarah found herself longing for tomorrow's commonplaces, for the gently metallic taste of an aroused nipple in her mouth.

"What was wrong with you?" asked Candy next morning.

"Nothing I can explain."

"Try not to be so insecure."

Sarah would have snapped off a retort, but a revelation silenced her. Exactly as Sarah once had she could see that Candy had grasped how impossible happiness was. And how fungible by everyday diversions.

lthough she expected Henry to call, Rebecca felt relief at his restraint. Huge and echoey on an upper floor in a brick Romanesque, her apartment share on the Upper West Side made her unreasonably happy. Her Dalton pals had taken entry level jobs in publishing; Alfonso, the brother of her Harvard friend, worked as a junior executive for a movie studio. The city where she had lived her entire life and to which she was linked by fifteen generations of Van Rijns had refreshed itself as a long-term proposition.

"So what happened to your boyfriend?" asked Laura at a dinner party. She and her husband, Bo, now an investment banker at Lehman Brothers, had bought an adult apartment in a pre-war co-op on 79th Street and Madison.

"Yeah," said Bo. "The baseball player."

"Did you dump him?"

The dinner party had been nice, although slightly stodgy. Several boys she had grown up with had put on weight and lost hair and two of the girls seemed prematurely mommified.

"Dump him? Not exactly. We're still friends."

"Wow!" said Bo. "Man overboard."

"What happened?"

"Nothing happened, we just decided to cool it."

"... and getting smaller and smaller in the distance."

"This is the guy you were going out with last summer?" asked Billy Hoyt, who had once when they were teenagers drunkenly tried to get Rebecca to put her hand down his pants. "The one you two were constantly in the papers for?"

"Yes, Billy, it was," she said.

By the end of the evening, Rebecca could no longer deny she was bored. When her cab burst through the transverse, she felt in need of Henry and his square-peggishness in her round hole world.

Alfonso had invited over a handsome young producer who spoke with a slight lisp. Alfonso's ex-girlfriend, Wilma, sat on a couch with Rebecca's cousin, Rex.

"Laura's," she said. "And where were you?"

"You need your own life."

Wilma, an almost-beautiful Cuban blonde, smacked Rex on the arm. "She's your cousin. Show some respect, instead of sarcastic all the time."

Rebecca laughed helplessly. "See?"

Scowling behind Wilma's back, Rex pulled the girl to his chest in a way that illuminated to Rebecca a home truth about men. Physical touch, specifically sex, was for them a refuge from disdain. Children replaced sex as the distractor and then divorce replaced marriage once the children grew up. Ugh, she thought, not looking forward to any of this.

"So what are you going to do for an encore," asked the pretty-boy producer. "Work on a farm? How about the professional bowling tour."

"I bet you spend your whole day rearranging your desk."

"Right on the button. But you have to come watch."

"Where's your office?"

"Gulf and Western Building. I'm serious, though. I'm working with a writer where we slide ashtrays the length of a table in the conference room. Whoever comes closest to the edge wins. We'll get you pom-poms and a twirl skirt so you can cheer us on."

She liked not knowing whether he was gay or not. Funny and high-energy, he appealed to her as exactly the type of experience she was now able to enjoy. But later, lying in bed, buzzed on a joint and half a can of beer, she revisited her relationship with Henry, mildly disturbed by its wrong-end-of the-telescope feel.

"God, I hope I'm not rushing myself," she said to Millie that Sunday afternoon.

"To do what?" asked her aunt.

"Have all my adventures so I can get married." Rebecca glanced at the Women's Finals of the US Open, which they were watching with Clara, who was now in the other room on an endless telephone call.

"Well, I liked him. But, you know, 'Becca, it's all just luck." Millie looked up as Clara entered, upset.

Clara waved her hand dismissively. "Neil." Crossing to the drink caddy, she mixed herself a martini while staring at her view of the East River. Aunt Clara had been divorced twice. Neil was a widowed socialite who no one in the family particularly liked.

"You should call the boy occasionally, 'Becca."

Clara looked over, curious what they were talking about, then not. "There's plenty of this." She indicated the shaker. Nodding at the television, she said, "Who's winning?"

Leaving her aunts to their martinis, Rebecca decided to drop in on her grandparents unannounced. They could be in Rhinebeck, of course, but she sought a touchstone in this tricky moment of reduced horizons.

At the apartment she discovered her grandfather had stayed in town to conclave with Sarah, that lawyer friend of Henry's. The clang of coincidence put her on alert. Livingston stood up from his 18th century desk, scads of legal documents peeled back like autopsy subjects. Unusually demonstrative, he kissed her on the cheek, leaving Rebecca to surmise that these documents concerned bequeathals and trusts.

"Rebecca, this is Miss Mortensen. She works with Myron Kandel. They've been updating our wills."

"Myron has," said Sarah, "I'm just the messenger girl."

"Miss Mortensen has been very helpful with some of these issues." He paused. "Do you two know each other?"

"Through a mutual friend," said Sarah.

"A lawyer?"

"No, grandfather. You met him. Henry Birdsall."

"Yes, I think so. The Princeton boy."

"More like man."

"I didn't expect to see you. Is everything going well? Grandmother will be pleased. Rebecca is living over on the West Side now with some friends," he said to Sarah.

"What street?"

"Eighty-third and Columbus. Where's Harriet?" she asked, needing an exit line.

Told to check Harriet's room, Rebecca muttered to Sarah a bleakly chipper say-hello-to-him-for-me, and finding Harriet in the kitchen asked, "How long has she been here?"

"This I do not know. But the cook, she is here for your grandfather's dinner."

"You know who she is, don't you? Remember Henry?"

"*Henri?* Where has he been?"

"They're friends or something."

"Should I tell Hildegard you will stay?" Rebecca shook her head. Guilt welled up at deserting her grandfather to his lonely meal. "I don't think he expects you to," added Harriet.

"I'm going out tonight with a group of people."

"She is a lawyer, this woman? With Mr. Kandel?"

"It surprised me."

Harriet put her hand on Rebecca's arm. "Go with your friends. Your grandfather? He will be busy tonight. And so, dinner on his tray."

With a hollowness of heart masked by resolve, Rebecca stepped into an understated Park Avenue dusk. Lawyers, wills: the unhappiness, implied and actual, among her aunts; law school; a future composed of legal documents like those on her grandfather's desk... Henry was the least of her problems. Excited as she was by her current life, she longed for her thoughts to gather on the subject of where she was headed, and with whom.

When the feds handed up indictments against members of the Lucchese family and others in the "mob-dominated concrete industry," Ray called Henry. "You knew about this."

"Yeah. Where'd Larry Park go after Cross. I called Merrill Lynch. Either they have no idea or they aren't telling me."

"Are you in the bottom of a well?"

"What? Oh, that. The number rings in the garage now."

"Do any of these charges have tails on them?"

"This concrete guy tipped me off on the bid-rigging. I told Sarah, who already knew. So back out to Queens I go, track down the guy in a diner. He acts like it's banquet seating and he never saw me before. Okay, mission accomplished. But, honestly, did I know Dicko was rigging bids? Besides the union bribes and check-kiting? No, I did not."

Listening to Henry, Ray decided to enlighten Dora tonight on the TeleMark disaster. Once a Hong Kong firm introduced a similar printing technology, the TeleMark IPO, already diving for the bottom, took a depth charge hit. When it was further revealed that one of its director had a stock fraud record under another name, Ray entertained pump-and-dump suspicions. But upon hearing that Drew Case had lost close to half a million on *his* roll of the dice, Ray could not muster sufficient fury to contact the SEC.

"We need to talk," he said to Dora after dinner.

"Yes, we do."

He followed her into the library. "Where are they?"

"Doing their homework. Ray, Melissa wants to study for the rabbinate. Has she told you yet?"

Despite first interpreting this news as a sign from God to postpone the TeleMark discussion, Ray soon saw the link between issues. In fact, Judaism demanded that the spiritual hold dominion over the pursuit of wealth. Magnanimously, he conceded, "Well, Melissa has always been the serious one."

"Actually, Karen is."

"They both are."

"My feeling is we shouldn't stand in her way. Although I admit I'd envisioned something different for her. More in the med school line."

"Me, too. You're sure this isn't a phase?"

"I'm not, but I've made enquiries and I think we should proceed. The Yeshiva will be more expensive. Naturally, she doesn't qualify for a scholarship."

Ray took a deep breath. "Let me just say: this is important. The schooling? This, we do not cut back on. Whatever happens, the girls come first. You and I will get by."

"What do you mean, 'whatever happens?'"

"I'll work two jobs. Melissa wants the rabbinate? Karen does, too? Then that's what they'll have. We lost some money on a public offering, honey."

"Oh, Raymond, for God's sake!"

"Three hundred grand," he said quickly, "but it reduces our tax exposure."

"Don't ever do this again."

"It was an insider price. I should have said no."

"What are we looking at?"

"A second mortgage."

"For household expenditures? You're an asshole, Ray!"

"True." But Ray took heart from the tone of her voice.

At the breakfast table, he counseled Melissa to ask Jahweh whether He really needed her to be a rabbi. His use of the word "Jahweh" drew snickers from the girls and an eye-roll from Dora, but his controlled buffoonery restored him to grace.

From the same business school classmate who held the Chemical Bank mortgage on the house, Ray arranged a second mortgage, having providentially boosted his stock there by alerting the banker, once the cat was out of the bag, about Dicko Fitzgerald's check kite. Deciding to remain mounted on his TeleMark stock until year-end, Ray watched other issues in his modest portfolio ski-jump in value. But he did cancel his subscription to that new business magazine, *Manhattan, Inc.*

"You're coming in tonight?"

"I was going to. But can we afford it?"

"Do you want to have dinner with Birdsall and his new girlfriend? She's a filmmaker or something."

"Not expensive, Ray. And not that terrible Irish place."

Birdsall had picked a trendy Japanese restaurant on the West Side, which Ray agreed to only after Henry announced his intention to treat. On the way there Ray and Dora engaged in a dispute over bus versus cab to save money. Conveyance by cab won, but only after it became clear to Ray that the new rules on family expenditures were to be administered by his wife.

The Japanese hotspot featured mirror-topped tables and pinlighted flower arrangements. When Henry arrived with his girlfriend, Ray had the deja-vu sense they had been together years. Henry could not stop touching the girl. "I think he wanted our approval," Ray said on the train home.

"I don't think he needs it," said Dora.

But Ray had been struck by this Nina Murray, Irish more by implication than by type despite the thick reddish hair and bisque complexion. French, he would have said, except for the directness of her gaze. She was smart and paid attention and did not wear her achievements on her sleeve. What surprised Ray most, however, was her very un-Irish warmth. Not charm, not wit, not mellifluous sentiment, but warmth. "What are we celebrating," he said, finally, "besides you two."

Henry lifted his glass. "We open next week. And we have another backer apart from you," he said, winking at Ray.

Ray fielded Dora's alarmed glance. "That's a joke, Dora."

Lawrence Park pulled up a chair. "Here's to Larry," said Henry, toasting his fellow sufferer at Armor Technical, who was now a successful stockpicker at Bear, Stearns.

"I like to diversify," explained Park on his decision to loan Birdsall a hundred grand. "I may even buy in."

Struggling to feel proud of his former subordinates, Ray eventually achieved a put-upon *paterfamilias* pose. "I hope you two will still visit your old Dad when you're rich and famous."

"Ray, Nina made that incredible documentary on PBS about Peru. The mine cave-in. Remember?"

"Actually, it was a strike," said Nina.

"How did you get those frightening-looking people to participate?" Dora asked. "Remember, Ray? You came in while I was watching. It was all in black-and-white."

"Mostly black-and-white. Sometimes it's easier being a woman. The wives talk to you. You hang around long enough, the men get curious."

"One of my girls," Dora said, "wants to be a rabbi."

"Congratulations."

Park, Birdsall and Nina took a cab downtown, Birdsall now essentially living with the girl. "That was quick," said Ray in reference to Henry's altered living arrangements.

"You told me how fast it all moves when you're ready."

Ray did not recall making any such remark.

As he and Dora caught a negotiated crosstown bus, she said, "You should be proud, Ray, even though I know you're not. They're almost like your sons."

"God forbid!"

"I liked his girl."

"Do you have exact change? Because I don't."

As Ray watched Dora ransack her purse, the sense of having been deserted floated away, as did rancor at his bad luck. And also his yearning to be something other than what he was. Which was not an explorer but a stay-at-home exhorter, a cheerleader for those who went out into the world.

B obbie called. "Your mother thinks you've had a nervous breakdown."

"Why, because I broke up with Rebecca?"

"And now have another girlfriend."

"Are you coming up?"

"I might have to," she said.

She had caught Henry on one of his rare returns to his apartment. Nina's place had space, high ceilings and a view of vestigial gardens. But Henry knew he had to make up his mind. Nina had other suitors. A young columnist for the *Daily News*; a man-about-town speechwriter for Mario Cuomo, and a European film editor with ambitions to direct. All were snappy with success and to varying degrees exhibited the sort of male vitality Henry saw as his only strength.

One Sunday, playing for Al Scoville in the Westchester fall league, he found he could not pick up a ground ball. A double session of intensely pleasurable sex had disrupted his hand-eye coordination. Nina had detonated the surface of his skin and he was now a lost cause on the baseball field.

"For years now, whoever I got involved with, I wanted to marry," he said that night, "but you're the first girl I think I could actually live with."

"Not what I'm looking for," she said.

Several days later, she told him about her father.

"Every once in a while he'd say he wanted to be a writer, but, really, I think, it was more the idea. Whatever book he wanted to write he wrote with his life. He was completely there. In everything he did."

"So what did he do?"

"Worked on tugboats as a second mate. Trained fighters. He used to fight. Middleweight, I guess, when he was young. Worked as a doorman and a bartender. The smoking killed him, not the drink. Never a big drinker."

She went silent. Henry nodded consolingly.

"Loved animals," she said. "Dogs especially. But it was the joy he took. The sun coming up over the water, the parade of characters in the bar where he worked. He was in love with the everyday."

"And with you," Henry said.

"Not 'in' love, no. He loved us both, my mother and me. I just hope he knew how much I loved *him*."

Nina had shown Henry a blurry black-and-white picture of her father. This, though, was not the vision that came before him now. Instead, he saw a curly-haired, round-headed guy, thick-necked and strong, entranced by evening light on the chop of the Upper Bay. Nostrils flaring, grey eyes clear, the guy was loosely wishing he had the words to remember this by.

"I'm sure he knew."

"That I loved him? I hope so," she said.

By now she had finished the rough-cut of her Nicaragua footage and was thinking of going back."

"Please don't."

She rolled over. "Why not?"

"Because I need you," he said, having never, ever said this to another human being.

She laughed. "Then maybe I'll stay." But he knew she had not yet decided *what* to do.

His mother made a flying visit to the city under cover of consorting with an old college chum. Henry immediately called Bobbie in Ardmore, who, annoyingly, took two days to call him back. "Why's she doing this?" he asked his sister.

"Because her antennae tells her you're serious. By the way, you ever hear from the one I met?"

"Not much. Called the other day to see how I was. She knows I've got a girlfriend."

"I heard it went well."

"With Guinivere? Fuck you 'it went well.' If I tell you what happened, can you keep it to yourself? Why am I telling you? I know you can't. You can't, can you?"

"No."

"Okay, so we're on our way to a screening. The plan is we'll come by where she's staying and say 'hi.' So we walk out to the elevator afterwards and Nina says to me, 'You never told me your mother's in love with you.'"

Bobbie laughed. "I always felt like a bigamist. Married to whoever and married to them. Let me warn you, sport, they're crumbling up straw and putting it in their hair."

The tension between elation and wind-whipped despair drove Henry to fits of vacantness. "What are you doing down there?" May barked over the phone.

"Here at the garage? Counting receipts."

"For two hours? Get your butt up here and nail down the numbers on your coupon thing."

Later, Henry sat on his apartment couch. One decision would tie him to life with a woman he loved, who also loved her work. The other would return him to his family and eventually, perhaps, to a girl who might be a better fit. He had no model for the first choice and the second cranked up the suicide siren. But then a "memory" appeared of Nina's father, his face bright with happiness, one foot up on a tugboat prow. On his way to Nina's that night, Henry bought flowers. Her response to his proposal, which he took as a yes, was, "Are you kidding?"

Afterwards, as he lay on her bed, an inspiration struck him. Stress had reduced his powers of ratiocination to dream-like visions. The imagined response of his parents to his marriage found representation in a hissing ball of snakes. "Why don't we get married before we get married?"

Nina turned from arranging his flowers in a vase.

"Go down to City Hall," he said.

She smiled. "And keep it secret."

"Have the wedding, but we're already married."

The next day Henry returned to his apartment for a load of fresh clothes. The doorbell rang, and expecting Nina, he opened the door to Rebecca. "I don't have your new number and you're never in your apartment. Have you heard of these things called answering machines?"

"How are you?" he said. Nina would be there any minute. The plan was to go shopping for a wedding ring.

"There's a way I haven't been fair to you, okay? Can I sit down? Why are you so nervous?"

"What do you mean 'haven't been fair?'"

"It occurred to me that you were actually kind of brave, working at a job you didn't like, trying to go into business for yourself. How's that going, by the way? And not caring whether it was a good idea or not."

"Going well," he said. "Thanks."

"So did you ask me how I like living on the West Side?"

"I bet you're having fun."

"I am. But I don't want you running off half-cocked."

"Why? What have you heard?"

She shook her head but he saw what concerned her. Their break up, she believed, had pushed him into a rebound situation beyond the reach of common sense. She wanted him to realize that she was not a dream he had woken up from. That they could still be friends. And maybe, some day, more.

"Listen, it's good to see you," he said.

"You're okay, aren't you?"

"Yeah."

When she left, a familiar need to protect her stole over him, and then a sadness. Distracted during the jewelry store canvass with Nina, he finally owned up to having had a visitor. Nina was hurt, then furious.

"The same day we're looking for our wedding ring?"

Henry scrambled to weight the happenstance properly, to convince her of its true unimportance. Separate from his efforts Nina reached that conclusion herself and withdrew her temper. After all, Rebecca had been there first.

Buster and Guinivere arrived the following week. They decided on the Knickerbocker Club, as it was halfway between Henry's apartment and Nina's. The discovery of Henry's new living arrangement occasioned a muffled shock.

"What will you do with your furniture?" his mother asked.

"Sell it."

Her skin went papery with self-control. "What about grandmother's pieces?"

"I only have one."

"I thought you had more."

"We're taking you two to dinner," said Buster, "any place you want to go."

"So long as it's French," said Gwen.

Perhaps love of her own father made Nina solicitous of his, but she researched midtown French restaurants and found a place. At the table Gwen grilled her about her background. Evident to Henry and probably also to Nina was his mother's mounting dismay. "And you're Catholic?"

"Fallen away. After convent school."

Buster came to life. "What was that like?"

"About what you'd expect, but I managed to survive."

"Is your mother religious?"

"She's had her fill. Her sister is, though."

"Does your family get together often?"

"Buster," said Henry "why don't you ask Nina about her documentaries. She's spent time in Latin America. Didn't you go into business once with a guy from Peru."

"Venezuela. So, Henry," Buster said, "how goes your parking thing. You should have asked me for the money."

Henry closed his eyes.

"Oh, Henry, stop it!" snapped his mother.

"Is Bobbie coming up," he said

"Supposedly, she's already here," said Gwen.

Truly, though, Henry sorrowed for the anguish he had caused his parents. Correctly, they viewed Nina as a dynasty killer. And furthermore, a wife who would never be tractable.

"They won't accept me, you know," she said.

Lying on his back, Henry stared into darkness. "He said to me as you were saying goodbye to my mother, 'I liked how she looked straight at me when she shook my hand.'"

Nina sighed; he had expected her to laugh. "I'm supposed to see her tomorrow," she said, "for tea."

"He wants me to play tennis with him. Some men's club he belongs to. You see what I'm dealing with here?"

"Because you don't have a men's club of your own?"

"Exactly."

He pulled her over and she lay on his chest for a while. Later that night a wind squealed and shivered her tall industrial windows. In the penetrated darkness he felt a purpose swell. He could do this, he realized. It was the right thing to do.

"It's certainly far over," said his father as the cab, in a spray of gravel goosed itself back onto the West Side Highway. "What do they call this part of Manhattan?"

"Chelsea. The people parking their cars with us? Our vans ferry them back and forth to the subway stops."

"*After* they park, they have to take the subway?"

"Hey, Rios, how you doing?" said Henry. "Melchior, *como esta?* Would you look at all these cars. They come in over the GW or through the Lincoln Tunnel. We even get some from the Holland, who work in the garment center."

As they left Pier Parking, Inc., his father stopped to regard Henry's first entrepreneurial venture. "Well, I suppose you should be proud of yourself. What's your partner like?"

The unprepossingness of May and her office blunted Buster's tepid enthusiasm. Henry could see that he, May and the parking garage had been designated "colorful," his father's usual response when confronted with social classes lower than his own. Furthermore, Henry could sense that he had now been categorized by May as Henry Birdsall, trust fund lint-head.

"Tough neighborhood?" Buster asked on the street.

"You're a stranger," Henry said, eyeing a group of aggrieved adolescents. "Me, they've seen." He glanced at his watch. "Too late for tennis. Where's lunch?"

"First, I have to make a call."

Henry was surprised but unsurprised when his mother appeared at the Knickerbocker for his lunch with Buster.

"So you're ganging up on me."

"We wanted to talk. This seemed like a good time."

In a corner of the club dining room, Gwen and Buster exerted long legacies of fate-shaping skills on what they took to be the plastic identity of their son. "It isn't that we don't like her," said Gwen. "She seems to be a nice woman."

"Young woman. Don't you guys ever get tired of this?"

"Personally, I liked her very much," said Buster. "Honest, straightforward."

"Yeah, I know. And a firm handshake grip."

"Thank you. I'll just have the Cobb Salad," purred Gwen to the waiter. "I saw several on the way to our table. It looks delicious"

"More importantly," said Buster, "what do I want?"

"Probably the *tournedos.*"

"But getting back to the matter at hand," Buster said.

"Look," Henry's mother continued, "I know you were in despair over your break-up with Rebecca. But suddenly you're seriously considering marriage to a girl you've known how long? A few weeks?"

"Long enough."

"I mean, if you want, give yourself time with Nina," said Buster. "Fine. Maybe she's the one. But not long ago, let me remind you, Rebecca was the one."

"I thought she was."

"Then how do you know this one is? Forget that," said his mother, sensing a tactical dead-end. "She just doesn't seem to be, well, someone you belong with. A career woman. Not the same religion or social class. And she older than you are, I understand."

"Big deal. A couple years."

"Do you know if she even wants children?"

Henry, himself, did not want children. But grandchildren were not to be X-ed out of the equation without a fight. "She's Catholic, for Christ's sake."

"My point."

"You can't have it both ways, Gwen."

"He's right," Buster chipped in. "Henry, let's step back and look at this. I like her, don't mistake me. Even though I thought Rebecca was a better match for you."

"Yeah, I got that."

"This girl is just not special enough. She's nice, probably quite successful, but she's not special. And you are."

"I'm *not* special, okay, that's the whole point. Rebecca's the princess, but I'm not the prince. Really, I'm not."

"Yes, you are," insisted his father, "you are the prince."

"Please don't get married now," said Gwen. "Wait."

"I can't wait."

Leaving his parents, Henry felt none of the decisiveness, none of the relief that he had felt traveling down to City Hall on the subway, three days earlier, to marry Nina in a civil ceremony in the office of the Clerk of Court.

When Bobbie called later, Henry, feeling alone and harried, snatched up the phone, hoping it was Nina who was out timing her footage, whatever that meant.

"Who *is* this chick?"

"You're here, right?"

"Not at the fucking Knickerbocker. They're still lying there with cold compresses on their heads."

"Fuck 'em if they can't take a joke."

"That's my brave little man."

"And you should try not tripping home to Mommy and Daddy whenever shit goes bang."

"Yeah, well, you're not there yet, sport. Let's see how you deal with years of nuclear winter. Or however long it's gonna be before you hand the mitten to this girl. Ann, remember her? She thinks you have no idea who you are."

"So why are you defending them?"

"You're breaking up the family."

"Oh, God, where do I start with that."

"When am I going to meet her?"

"Not now. She's already had to endure Gwenny."

Hanging up, Henry attuned his hearing to every front door sound, until the rasp of key-in-lock mandated a casual pose.

Nina dumped film cans in a chair.

"How'd it go?" he said.

"You look a little tense."

"This is hard."

"I know." She seemed completely relaxed, however.

"They sandbagged me."

"So I heard. Look, we don't have to do this," she said.

"We already did it."

"It can be undone."

He shook his head. "What happened?"

She smiled. "What a scene. Her pal, that helmet-hair woman? She fled as soon as the tea arrived. Your mother got right down to it, though."

"More why-are-you-doing-this-to-me?"

"No, I mean right to the point. 'Leave my son alone.'"

"You're kidding?"

She did an imitation of his mother, not entirely malicious. "'We're a very close-knit family and nice as you are, you wouldn't fit in. I'm sorry, but that's how we feel. We know Henry wants children and you'll be too busy with your career for that. And, besides, this is so sudden. We actually thought Henry had suffered a nervous breakdown, that's how upset he was when he broke up with Rebecca. Next thing we know, he's engaged to you.'"

"What did you say?"

"I said, 'Take him back, you want him so much.'"

"God bless you! What did she do?"

"She kind of blinked a little. I said, 'He's no bargain.'"

"'I know he isn't,'" she said. "'Believe me, I do. But.'"

"'But' what?"

"That was it. 'But.' Some stuff about growing up in the West bonding all of you together. We said goodbye and I walked out. I think her friend's still hiding in the kitchen."

Henry embraced her. Distracted by her triumph she barely responded. She had slain the dragon. He had fought inconclusively and retreated. "I really *am* no bargain," he said.

"So how'd you do?" She opened the refrigerator. "We don't have to go out with them tonight, do we?"

"How did I do? I'm just glad we're already married."

"For a second, I think your mother saw the difference between who she thinks you are and who you really are."

"Remember my sister?"

"Not tonight," she said. "Please."

On the way to Soho late the following afternoon after a phone call from Buster pledging eternal unhappiness if this marriage went through, Henry warned Nina that his favorite sibling had joined the wrong cheering section. "Meanwhile, you have my mother," said Nina, "who actually likes you."

"I keep going back to the no-bargain concept."

Bobbie had selected for a rendezvous a decidedly nicked and dingy Prince Street bar. Swinging off a barstool, she jerked her thumb at an open table. "So I guess we all know who we are," said Henry as a waitress wiped off the tabletop.

One look at Nina, and Bobbie said, "Jesus, Henry, what's this? You're suddenly Mr. Hip and Happening?"

"Why, because she's in the arts? What'd you expect? A debutante? Nina, this is Bobbie."

"Hello," said Nina evenly.

"Oh, well," said Bobbie, sucking at a suspiciously dark ginger ale. "We need all kinds in the family."

"Bobbie's been holding a casting call."

"This is Willis and Jean," said Bobbie, looking up. "Sit down, kids." A gangly cadaverous male and his swaybacked girlfriend took chairs. "What happened to your buddy?" she said to Henry. "The one I was supposed to marry."

To Nina he explained, "She means the baseball guy, Al Scoville. Bobbie, how bad is it?"

"Bad. Sorry," she said to Nina. "They're up in arms."

"You think I give a fuck!"

"Christ, Bobbie," said Henry. But Nina was stalking out of the bar. Ears flaming, the semiotics of this little drama evident to the clientele, Henry followed her outside. October misted the cobblestones, streelights fuzzy as dandelions.

"Go back if you want," she said, "I'm going home."

"Look, she's being an asshole."

"Don't they know how fucking petty this is?"

"No, they don't. They should. But they don't."

"There's so much worse out there."

Nicaragua. Whatever horrors she had seen in Africa and South America. He admired her bigness and scope. It made him laugh. "Come on," he said.

"I thought you liked her."

"I do. But I like you better. Let's get this over with."

172

When Henry and Nina re-entered the bar, several barstool comedians clapped, which nearly reversed the established vector, Nina not wishing to appear tamed.

"These two want to get married," Bobbie announced, "and my family's giving them a hard time."

"Bobbie. Jesus. Enough. And quit drinking."

"Yeah," said Willis, as though testing his voice.

"Would you rather I did drugs?" Bobbie said.

"Get up to New York much?" Nina asked.

Bobbie chewed her lip. "Look you guys, they'll get over it. I mean, what are they gonna do? Boycott the wedding?"

"Actually, I could see that," said Henry.

"No, they'll come."

"Will you?" said Nina.

"Always up for a party," said Bobbie unconvincingly.

Decamping after a proper interval, Henry and Nina slept like the dead that night in the cemetery quiet of Lower Park Avenue. The next afternoon the parent/sibling trio took a cab to Penn Station, Henry and Nina showing up to wave goodbye.

"Help me, help me," mugged Bobbie from the back seat. "I'm being held against my will. Alert the police!" Her voice trailed away as the cab trundled off. "Rescue me. Pleeease…"

"You really think they'll skip the wedding?" Nina said.

"They'll keep trying to break us up between now and then. Believe me, they're not even thinking about the wedding."

"I don't know how much more of this I can stand."

"But you agree. I *am* the smartest man in the world. Married first, then 'married?'"

By late fall, Al had a structure in place for his City Council campaign. Rickshaw introduced him to Downtown people who knew people in Al's Upper West Side district. A storefront office on 108th and Broadway became his for negligible rent. From Candy, the paralegal, Al received a torchlight parade of law school students eager to envelope-stuff and knock on doors. Candy's girlfriend, the lawyer, Sarah Mortensen, connected him up with a political consultant over-qualified to run a City Council race but broke and available. The money started trickling in.

"I'm going for Council," he told Elizabeth. They had not spoken since his Los Angeles trip.

"That's good."

"You always said."

"I did, yeah And now you doing it. Seems a long, long time ago, though. Passed my real estate license."

"That's good, too." Al stared at his dogs, asleep on their floor cushions. "Outside of that, I'm pretty much unchanged."

In the white muzzles of his labrador and beagle, in the shrinking circumference of their nighttime walks, Al sensed the implacability of death and began to see his political aspirations as a bargaining attempt. His dogs would die, he would become too old to hit a baseball, his urge to express himself sexually would fade. He would expire, a lonely bachelor. Primaries loomed in June. Three more candidates had entered the race: a white lawyer backed with West End Avenue money, a PTA woman with an impressive network of connections, and a mysterious businessman parachuted in by well-heeled invisibles.

"So what do you think?" Birdsall asked his new girlfriend.

"It could be interesting, sure."

"You could film it over a number of years if he wins."

The girl nodded.

"Supposing I don't want no part of this," said Al.

Now she smiled.

Through the window of his campaign office, Al spotted Birdsall and the girl arguing on the sidewalk. The veins stuck out on Birdsall's neck, but his girlfriend stood her ground. To one of his campaign workers Al nodded at the window. "He's pissed she don't want to make a movie out of me."

"Why not?" said the kid.

"But it ain't what they're really fighting about. He's trying to get her to shoot something in the city. So she don't take off somewheres else. You leaflet 96th Street?"

"Yes, I did."

Al regularly checked receipts at the Herb Garden, but the efficiency of his manager, Lacy Cho, presumed his irrelevancy. A Korean reared in the Bronx, she had relatives in greenmarkets and in a new phenomenon, nail salons. "You get elected, you sell the store to me," she said.

Al's mother and sister had returned years ago to South Carolina. Reared on these streets, but with none of his people here, he felt uprooted by newcomers willing to feed two generations into assimilation's fire. Lying on his fold-out bed, he saw himself as a ghost in the making, fated to complete incorporeally whatever it was his purpose had been here on earth. "You really want to do this?" asked Herbie Maes, his campaign manager.

"Doing it for my health, you think?"

"Sometimes I don't know what you're doing it for."

Herbie's acne scars stipulated adolescent suffering, but the man had achieved grace as a curtain-puller for the well- formed. Al was circumstance to him, nothing more. A scholar of voting trend ephemera, he had an instinct for ambivalence and sensed anger and desperation in Al.

"Ladies and gentlemen, seniors, kids. Anybody I left out? Glad to be here tonight at the Riverside Community Center to tell you a little bit about myself and where I'm coming from. But, mostly, to find out about you. What's concerning you, what you feel our neighborhood needs from City Hall. I'm gonna convince you I'm the right candidate to take your voices Downtown, the one gonna make it so you heard."

Al looked out at the assembled haircuts; at the flock of empty chairs; at the two basketball players in sweat-baggy socks lounging in the doorway. His presence here seemed arbitrary. A lack of interest in his own interests extended to the interests of every face in the room. Often in the Q&A quacking over matters of local import, his hearing and eyesight would fade. Tonight he even fainted.

"It's okay, give him air. Nothing to eat all day."

Eyes closed tightly he wished for an extension of this lightless reprieve, but eventually had to admit to murmurs of concern, "I'm fine." Helped to his feet, handed a soft drink, Al suddenly understood how the solicitude of others could render solitude intolerable. Al, the needy, took form that night.

"I feel energized," he told Herbie.

"Well, energize on some more soda and a bite of this."

"I'm serious," said Al. "I'm getting the hang of it."

Which got a laugh. But he waited to reveal what he meant until he walked Candy, the paralegal, home. "Trick is, I take care of them, they'll take care of me."

"Meaning what?" Candy asked. "By 'take care of?'"

"They'll invade my life. Which needs invading."

"People look up to you, Al."

"Because I'm tall. Here's my thinking. Whole idea is be busy so you lifted up when them big changes come."

They walked in silence for a block, Al continuing mutely to pontificate. "Changes, yes," Candy said finally.

"All that talking back and forth? People gathering to hear someone might do 'em some good? It's a form of love."

"I'm still thinking about 'changes,'" Candy said. "What it is is we make 'em so they don't just happen to us."

"Correct. How's the other lady?"

"She's doing fine," Candy said. They had reached the building where her girlfriend lived. "Sends her best."

When Al got home, Benji, his labrador, trembling and white in the gums, could not stand up. Al carried him to a cab, leaving Al, the beagle mournfully alone. Over to the East Side, to the Animal Medical Center, where lumped among a sleepy sorrowing clientele, Al sat for two hours waiting for Benji's test results. Grief came to him like a hammer blow. Finally, the young vet willowed out from the back with Benji on a cotton hospital leash.

"Blood pressure's low, but his count's fine. Might have a tumor, but we can't find it on film. Check back with us tomorrow. And give him this. I've written a prescription."

Beside himself with happiness, Al took the leash.

"We had him on IV. He's doing a lot better."

Riding home in a cab with Benji, who lay on the back seat, his eyes reacting to varying intensities of streetlighting, Al vowed to give up his new calling and devote himself to his two dogs for what remained of their lives. He could not survive, he feared, the death of even one of them. Once he arrived home, Al, the beagle, woke up. Stiff-legged over to Benji. Sniffed his mouth and tail. Satisfied, went back to his cushion after a wag for Al and a muted bark. Benji, weak, and with many sensations to digest, slumped on his own cushion, open-eyed. In the darkness Al lay on his fold-out and wept.

R ebecca had decided on law school, which meant selecting which school she preferred. Her grades at Harvard had been that good.

Clara and Diana were surprisingly undemonstrative.

Aunt Millie asked, "Are you sure this is what you want?"

Laura tried to hide her jealousy and then said Bo thought business school would be the better choice.

Her other cousins, Rex, Tony, Annette, Jenny, et al, acted politely unimpressed. Her grandmother was benignly pleased, but Grandfather Livingston sat her down for a talk.

"I have no doubt that those many generations of lawyers in the family may have predisposed your decision," he said. "However, if you are lucky and the law does not come to you naturally, you will be improved by your efforts. The assembled body of precedent is a thing of beauty."

"Sounds good," she said. "No, seriously, grandfather, probably I want to be a lawyer because of you."

Now that her big decision had passed under her prow, her thoughts eddied around Henry again. Although her circle and his did not intersect, she had received reports that he and his filmmaker girlfriend had become seriously involved.

Under the pretext of asking law school advice, Rebecca arranged to have lunch with Sarah Mortensen at a steakhouse in midtown. Appalled by Sarah's intentional undecorativeness, Rebecca vowed, once she became a lawyer, not to throttle her femininity through clothing choices.

"Yale for theory, Harvard for practice, Columbia for New York," said Sarah.

"Where did you go?"

"The University of Michigan."

"Should I apply there?"

"You could. It's a very good school. As is Boalt."

"Berkeley? I have half a mind to. Totally new for me. California might be fun. Adventure, *c'est moi*."

Sarah allowed herself a small smile.

The pauses, the considered statements, the concise way of speaking, these struck Rebecca as lawyerly mannerisms she might do well to learn. "What do you hear from Henry."

"Henry Birdsall?" said Sarah. "Not much."

"So you don't know whether he's happy with this girl."

"Have you met her?"

"I hear rumors they got married."

"Can I pass on some advice about advice? As a lawyer remember that your personal opinions may push the wrong lever in a client. Give options, let the client chose. Therefore, pay little attention to what I say about Henry."

"I miss him in ways that don't add up to love."

"Go on," said the lawyer.

"He needs more seasoning."

Sarah, unexpectedly, laughed.

Rebecca laughed, too.

"Where on earth did that come from?" she said. "I don't know, maybe we make the kind of pattern where the stitches touch, separate, then touch again. Let me put it another way. I can't tell yet if I'm supposed to be with him.'

"I think Henry's the type who will never settle down."

"What about the girl?"

"I don't know. I liked her."

"But you won't say I made a mistake. Dumping him."

"I couldn't even guess. Management consulting seemed to suit Henry. He could glide from posting to posting without ever lowering his landing gear."

When they parted outside the restaurant, Rebecca felt Sarah had been studying her as a exemplar of what it meant to be young. As she watched this corporate lawyer vanish into the sidewalk swarm of pedestrians, she was visited by a tumble of images from her months with Henry. Unassailably specific, they now constituted her past.

Thanksgiving, as always, convened available clan in

Rhinebeck at her grandparents' estate. The weather was warm enough for the traditional touch football game to be played barefooted. By Rebecca, among others.

"Weren't you cold?" Diana asked.

"I had to. My tennis shoes were slipping."

"So?" said her aunt. In the windows of the porch the weather was now true November. A fire gurgled in the grate.

"Yale. That's my first choice."

"Oh, God, poor grandfather."

"Well, I haven't gotten in yet."

"Rebecca, whatever happened to that boy?"

"'That boy,' Diana?"

Diana freshened her goblet of wine. "Do you know why it didn't work out with him? Henry, right?"

"Why?"

"Don't take this badly, please. It's because of who you are. Anyone you're with, Rebecca, automatically becomes special. Just being plain old rich can do the same thing, by the way. And of course you're never quite sure what people like you for." Diana paused. "Someone who actually *is* special might be easier for you. People who *want* to be special might find themselves eventually, but not attached to you."

"So I should marry a tycoon."

"That's not what I said."

"You're saying you never felt he was right for me?"

"Except I didn't feel that way."

"Then why are you saying it now?"

"Because it strikes me as true."

"I'll remember that if I end up with him. He'd probably agree with you. He wasn't too bad at seeing himself."

"And you miss that. Which I can understand."

"I think I do," Rebecca said, staring out the window.

She sighed and abandoned her chair for a warm shower upstairs. That night, having coffee in the drawing room with an assortment of relatives, she experienced in her chest a sinking sensation, followed shortly by the buoyancy of release, which later she identified as happiness.

Returning before New Year's from a visit home, Sarah found in her mail an invitation to *A Party to Celebrate the Wedding of Henry Birdsall and Nina Murray.* "When'd you get married?" she asked over the phone.

"Couple months ago. How's Candy? Still working with Al? His dog died, you know."

"We broke up."

"That's a shock. I didn't know you were together."

"Yes, you did."

"Why'd you break up? I mean, should I be sorry?"

"Don't fuck around."

"Okay, I'm sorry then."

"I'm not. It was time. But invite her, we're still friends." After the snowbanks of Elmira, the overheated cheeriness of her parents house, Sarah rejoiced at being back in the city.

"Had you two been fighting? Although fighting can be good, I think. I hope. What happened?"

"Things hadn't been going that well. She went home to Chicago, decided not to come back. She's young, Henry. They don't always find their way first time out of the box."

Her brother, Tim, knew about Candy, and her parents had guessed. Sarah smiled, thinking how the subject of her "orientation" might have been discussed: a lobster volleyed back and forth between tennis racquets.

An hour later she glanced up from her escritoire to discover the sycamore limbs across the street veined with snow. The intimate rhythm of tire chains in the applied quiet now filtered into her consciousness. On the flight home, she had trapped the glance of a tired-eyed, generously featured blonde who emanated a quiet willingness to throw her life away. Sarah had been elated. Youthful ambition had made Candy brittle. Sarah needed a woman old enough to have disavowed fear. In her mother that quality of at-home-in herself had been a revelation.

On her way down to the bar rented for the occasion, Sarah amused herself by wondering if Candy might fly in from Chicago. Definitely in attendance would be Al Scoville, whose political campaign she had once accused Candy of using as a pretext to resume her heterosexuality. Wrong about that, yes, but also right, as the hurly-burly of local politics had reawakened in her young lover a desire to involve herself in the civic affairs of her hometown.

The bar reminded her, unavoidably, of Dean's. The shadowed gaiety struck her as appropriate to the event, but the predominance of strangers led her to assume a separation of realms between bar crowd and wedding party. Then she noticed Ray Levin chatting with the bartender and the bride herself accepting congratulations from a barstool party of four. Evidently, the entire establishment had been rented out. Ray kissed Sarah on both cheeks. "Where's your wife," she said.

He jerked his head toward the dining section. Several tables were crowded and voluble; others, sparsely inhabited by incommunicados.

"Where's the groom?"

"Wandering around shell-shocked." Alcohol and elation rosied Ray's features. "His parents haven't said two words to the bride's mother. Not two words. Her father's dead, did you know that? Here, say hello to her. Nina?"

Turning, Henry's wife smiled. "Sarah, the lawyer. We could have used you. They wanted me to sign a pre-nup."

The girl had distance in her voice. Supple and fine was her figure in that tight, off-white dress. She exuded, though, the air of being costumed, even scripted. Sarah could imagine her wishing to be rid of this ceremonial emptiness and alone with her new husband. In privacy her avidity would bloom.

"I hope Henry stood up for you," Sarah said.

"He did. I'm glad you came." Nina glanced over at a table where a woman conversed with a bored little girl.

"Is that your mother?"

"It is."

Sarah approached the woman. "I'm Sarah Mortensen, a friend of Henry's."

"Regina Murray. Sit down."

Regina rallied interest when Sarah mentioned the name of her firm. Regina's own job brought her into contact with the wheels-within-wheels world of Shea, Gould. In fact, she had known Bill Shea, the name partner, as a young man. Nina soon swept over, pulling a kite string of bride's-side family to attach to her mother. Thank you, she nodded to Sarah.

After this, the evening blurred. Cater waiters kept the trays of champagne swerving through the gathering. "This must have cost you plenty," Sarah said to Henry.

"Not too bad. Nina's mother knows the bar owner. Nina uses the caterers on commercial shoots and I got a break on the booze. Come here." Pale and stressed, Henry steered her to a table where sat, among others, a regal-looking couple. His mother, small, dark and fine-featured, looked up at Henry.

"This is Sarah Mortensen," he said. "She could have put me in jail but didn't."

"Henry, why do you say things like that?"

"Because," he said.

Al Scoville, glancing up at Sarah, nodded.

"Nice to meet you," said Mrs. Birdsall, with perfect punctilio. "I'm Guinivere, Henry's mother. And this is my husband... Buster?" The man she indicated, heavy-shouldered with a leonine head, had wrinkled his nose up at a slice of wedding cake.

"This has chocolate in it."

"Eat it, Bus," said a big blond girl. "Bad luck not to."

"Good, then I won't. Nice to meet you," he said to Sarah. "Have you met Al Scoville? Say, Al."

"Yes, I have," she said.

"Al, I got a question for you," said Buster, but the baseball coach had drifted off with Henry. "I wanted to ask him about Philadelphia," he explained to Sarah.

"So you must be a lawyer," said Guinivere. "Are you a

friend of Nina's?"

"Henry's."

"Of course."

"Grab a chair, May," boomed Buster Birdsall.

"The hell with it, I'd rather stand. You're dead meat you sit down," said a squat, tough-looking woman, snatching a champagne flute from a passing tray. "Pretty good stuff," she said to Sarah. "He got it through a pal of mine. Who are you?"

"We talked on the phone. Sarah, the lawyer, remember? Not-Jewish Sarah."

"Is that right?" said the woman vaguely. Moments later, she pulled Sarah aside. She had a grip like a weight-lifter. "Is this kid gonna prove out? And he's not exactly a kid. Although so far, so good, I have to say."

Spiritless dancing followed unfunny toasts and the steady attrition of party-goers to family-obligation-fatigue. At one point, Sarah spotted Henry talking to his dissipated sister and well-fed older brother, whose wife was predictably pert. Nina approached the group, but aborted the mission when Birdsall parents joined the Birdsall siblings. In Henry's flight to the side of his wife, Sarah read a changed loyalty.

Sarah picked off Al Scoville on his way out the door.

"Was she helpful to you?"

"I dropped out. She's moving on, I heard."

"You're not running?"

"Gave back the money. But staying on at the Community Board. Maybe another time," he said without conviction.

Watching Al depart, Sarah remembered Candy taking her hands. Remembered two sets of arms swinging back and forth, girlhood haunting this hard adult task. Huge effort by Sarah had forced reconsideration but not concession. When the cord cutting call from Chicago came, a propulsive sentimentality triggered more of her anger than she would have liked to admit. Ray intercepted her at the coat check. "This is Dora," he said.

"This is Dora who's driving him home," said his wife.

"I'm budgeting for a hangover, too," said Sarah.

"Tell me you're not going in tomorrow!"

His wife looked perplexed. "Of course she's not, Ray."

But, of course, she was. Going in.

Her coat already on, Sarah fell prey to the brothers Lynch. "Anything you could tell us would be appreciated," said the wife of the dark-haired brother.

"About the prosecution," erupted the freckled pale-eyed Lynch. "We're at a wedding, for Christ's sake!"

"So anything you've heard. Okay?"

Through the brain-tinsel of champagne Sarah fumbled the link together. Nina's uncle, Hugh, the other defendant in the concrete case. "Did your father come tonight?" she said.

The dark-haired brother laughed.

"His wife came," said the daughter-in-law.

"Did you know we introduced them?" said her husband.

"I'm not a prosecutor anymore. But I will tell you this. At certain historical periods, mob defendants can be notoriously difficult to convict. We're in one of those periods."

"Well, what a relief," said the freckled one nastily.

The wife shot Sarah a half-friendly scowl and then, prowly as bears, the three Lynches departed. Henry took her by the elbow. "God, I'm tired. You see your boyfriend?"

She glanced over at the bar. The Mediterranean-looking guy, the actual occupant of the office Birdsall had poached, was helping his wife on with her coat. "Hey!" said the man, "Freddy Habyan. Nice to see you again, dear."

Sarah willed his gaze upward from her bust. His wife sighed. "Freddy, say goodnight to your little friend and let's go." She patted Henry on the cheek. "Good luck, sweetie. This one's constantly regaling me with stories about you."

Moments later, Henry walked Sarah out. Coatless, he shivered in the December night. "Thanks for coming," he said, shaking her hand. Having passed through a membrane into the next chamber of his life, his voice seemed to echo.

For her part, Sarah had accepted her own singularity and was fully content.

In the spring Henry embarked on a tour of the wreckage he had indirectly caused. The impulse came to him while scanning a *Daily News* article about the upcoming Lucchese trial. Richard Fitzgerald III and Hugh Lynch were mentioned prominently. On the same page, another article noted the failed appeal by Artie Machado to reverse his guilty verdict in the Armor Technical case.

"This is a sign," Henry said.

At her desk May Roehmer, on the phone with a lawyer, hung up with a bang. "These cocksuckers will consider our bid, he says. That's all, 'consider.' 'A sign' of what? Have you paid that guy back yet?"

"Larry? Almost. May, there's other parking lots for sale, let's not obsess. And what about my floating barge idea?"

"Do not bring that up again. Are you mental? 'A sign' of what, goddamnit."

"Nothing. But here's something. I'm going with Nina to Nicaragua to finish this damn documentary."

"For how long?"

"I'm freaked out, okay. It's a war zone. A month."

May laughed. "You told her you have a job

"Listen, I woke up last night, my heart was racing. It's more like three weeks I'll be gone. Three weeks to a month."

"So anytime she makes a movie, you go with her?"

"In a word, 'maybe.' Actually, in a word, 'yes.'"

"Not every time. This once, okay."

"Don't 'this once' me," he said, standing up.

"Where you going?"

"Down to the pier, deposit the cash."

"You're pissing me off, you know." She picked up the phone. "I'm calling Katsoulas direct. Fuck this lawyer."

Instead of trotting the cash over to the bank, Henry

withdrew his Fiat from the parking shed and headed for the Bronx. In these early months of marriage not infrequently had the image of Dicko et al returned to him with force, the check kite trial up and running in Criminal Courts.

Because Fitzgerald Sand & Stone had been placed in receivership, Henry expected to see tumbleweeds roaring across the workyard in the Bronx. Through hearsay supplied by Nina he knew that the Lynch brothers now worked construction. That Karen Mulroney was running the shop of a small concrete supplier on Long Island. That most of the trailer girls had scattered, including Molly, a housewife again in Queens.

"This does not fill me with joy, you know."

"Not all of them deserved it, but the main ones did."

"What does your mother say?"

"She's just glad you care what she thinks."

Now, as Henry approached the Bronx plant, emotion tightened his hands and neck. Two transit mixers stood in the yard. A few cars lined the weedy margins. Then a door opened in one of the trailers and Pete McCann shambled down the steps. Henry pulled in and parked.

"What the fuck," he said.

Pete shook his head. "Not so unusual."

"Now that I think of it, no. Receivership. But they still have to run the place."

"You knew about the bid-rigging?"

"Not really. But you did, didn't you?"

"They tell you that bullshit Santa story?"

"Yeah, Molly. Nina said she wasn't sure."

Pete laughed. "So, I hear you got married."

"We could have used you at the party. I kissed the ground when I got off *that* plane, believe me."

"Walk me over, I got work to do." They headed for one of the transit mixers. "I wasn't cut out for cop. The money sucks and I tried to implement. Basically, doing the same thing every day calms me down."

"I'm beginning to feel like that."

"Except you won't."

"What do you mean?"

Pete climbed up into his cab, rolled down the window. His look of mild regret touched Henry. "You'll do something with yourself. Like Nina has."

At Armor Tech the padlocked factory gates and holes in the window panes did not affect Henry, but the tin barn where the pontoons and ladders had been fabricated plunged him into an agitated gloom.

A mother and two kids walked by, the boy hashing at the pavement with a stick. A car passed slowly, two men inside, fastidiously ignoring him. A sign to leave, quick. Henry dallied, though, until again the car approached. Without another glance at the abandoned factory, he roared off at speed.

Back at the parking shed, he drifted onto the catwalk at the edge of the pier. Wiping dry the slats of his junkyard chair, he sat down. The iciness of the river air would not permit him much time out here.

"This way I won't have to hire an assistant," Nina had said, once the idea of Henry coming with her to Nicaragua had been agreed upon. "Besides, you need to travel. See the world."

"I think I do, yes," said Henry with a sinking heart.

"It'll be fun."

"Possibly."

Chaos and death squads, disgraced fascists plotting *coup d'etat* in the hills. The Spanish language. In the *sturm und drang* pursuant to his choice of mate, he had realized how finding the right wife only prepared him for usefulness. Did not constitute usefulness itself.

Now, perched over the river, he achieved that moment of synaptical confusion which always gave him such delight. The Hudson, stationary, the island of Manhattan, moving.

Grinning, he stood up and went back to work.

THE END